MW01591031

The Last Shiba

Copyright © Harjeet Ryatt 2025

www.thelastshiba.com

This is a work of fiction. Names, characters, places, and events are either the product of the author's imagination or are used fictitiously.

Cover artwork generated using AI (Midjourney).

First Edition

ISBN: 9798296612533

Acknowledgments

Writing a story like this is never a solitary journey.

This story wouldn't exist without the love, encouragement, and insight of those closest to me. To my family and friends—thank you for the encouragement, support, and quiet belief that helped bring this story to life. Every kind word, every moment of feedback, and every bit of patience meant more than I can express.

To **Paddington**, my loyal Shiba Inu—this story is, in so many ways, a reflection of you. And to **Juggy**, my first dog and beloved Staffordshire Bull Terrier—you and Paddington have been part of two very different times in my life, yet both have shown me the same unwavering loyalty and love that only a dog can give.

You are more than pets. You are family, and this story carries a part of both of you.

"The world may break, but loyalty doesn't.
Not when it walks beside you."

Prologue: The Breaking of Time

The world ended not with a roar, but with a silent unraveling—a slow, unavoidable tearing of reality's seams. In the years that followed, survivors would whisper of a day when time itself began to fracture, when the steady rhythm of past, present, and future collapsed into chaos. No one had foreseen it, and no one truly understood it until the scars remained etched upon the land. In the days before the Breaking, humanity had been preoccupied with its own frailties. Wars, famine, and the relentless pace of modern life had left many disillusioned, yet none could have imagined that the very fabric of existence would one day come undone.

Scientists and mystics alike had debated the nature of time, each theorizing about its infinite layers, but never had they imagined that time would recoil against itself. Then came the Day of the Rapture—a moment when the sky fractured like a mirror dropped on stone. Glowing openings spread across the heavens, and the earth trembled under an unseen force.

In those final moments, reality splintered: echoes of the past intermingled with blurred visions of the future, and the steady march of time degenerated into a cascade of shattered moments. For some, the event was instantaneous, a single, breathtaking collapse; for others, it was a gradual descent into disarray, where each second stretched into an eternity of loss and confusion. In the aftermath, cities lay in ruins. Buildings that once reached proudly toward the sky were reduced to heaps of twisted metal and crumbling concrete. The once-familiar landscape was now a patchwork of anomalies— portions of history and fragments of the future coexisting in a discordant tapestry.

Time was no longer a linear path but a labyrinth of overlapping eras, each step forward fraught with uncertainty. Amidst this desolation, one figure moved quietly through the wreckage—a man named Ryo, hardened by loss and burdened by the weight of survival. Alongside him was his faithful companion, a Shiba Inu known simply as Kota.

From the moment Ryo brought home the puppy, a bond had formed that was as enduring as it was mysterious. Kota, with his keen eyes and unyielding loyalty, became more than just a pet; he was Ryo's constant in a world where even time had betrayed its promise. There were whispers among the survivors—rumours that certain beings possessed an inexplicable connection to the fractured timeline. Some called them "Timekeepers," others spoke of guardians hidden among the chaos. Ryo never paid much attention to such tales, focused as he was on simply surviving each day.

Yet, as the anomalies grew more frequent and more pronounced, it became increasingly clear that Kota was no ordinary dog. In moments of inexplicable calm amid the turmoil of the rifts, Kota's eyes would glimmer with an otherworldly light, and the air around him would vibrate ever so softly—like the distant echo of a long-forgotten melody. In the silent hours before dawn, when the broken fragments of time seemed to whisper secrets in the wind.

Ryo would sometimes catch a glimpse of something that defied explanation—a flicker of a memory, a flash of another life. These visions were as fleeting as they were unsettling, a reminder that the past was not entirely lost, nor was the future fully secured. Instead, all that remained was a mosaic of moments, scattered like shards on a cold, hard floor.

As Ryo journeyed through the desolation, each step carried with it the weight of what had been and the uncertainty of what might come.

The landscape was a testament to human hubris and nature's ultimate indifference; nature had reclaimed its domain with quiet determination, covering the scars of civilization with creeping vines and silent, persistent moss.

In the distance, the shattered remains of highways and overpasses served as stark monuments to a time when everything was different—a time when hope and despair had been measured in days and nights, not in fragments of lost time. For Ryo, every day was a struggle against both the external dangers of marauders, time anomalies, and the internal torment of memory and regret.

The broken clock of the world offered no solace—only a reminder that the past was irretrievably gone and that the future, if it existed at all, lay hidden behind an impenetrable veil of uncertainty. Yet in the midst of this chaos, a fragile hope endured. It was the hope embodied in the bond between a man and his dog—a hope that perhaps, through loyalty, sacrifice, and the sheer force of will, a new beginning could be forged from the remnants of a broken timeline.

Whispers of a destiny intertwined with Kota's very being began to circulate among those who still dared to dream. For if one creature could hold the pulse of time within him, maybe there was a chance to mend the shattered threads of existence. This hope, however, was tempered by a bitter truth: every miracle came at a cost.

The Time Rapture had not only fractured the continuity of existence but had also unmoored the very essence of what it meant to be human. In this new world, survival was not enough; one had to navigate the labyrinth of time itself, a challenge that demanded both courage and sacrifice. And so, in the twilight of a shattered era, the stage was set for a journey that would test the limits of endurance, faith, and the bonds that hold us together. Ryo, with his worn hands and weary eyes, stepped forward into the unknown, his faithful companion, Kota at his side, unaware of the role they were destined to play in the restoration of time.

The echoes of a bygone era mingled with the promise of a future yet to be written, as the fractured world waited—silent, watchful, and poised on the edge of a new dawn.

Chapter 1: Shattered World

Ryo crouched low behind a crumbling concrete wall, his heart pounding in rhythm with the distant echoes of a world long past. Dust swirled in the heavy afternoon air as sunlight filtered weakly through the fractured sky, casting distorted shadows across the ruins. He clutched his makeshift weapon—a sharpened metal pipe—with white-knuckled determination. Beside him, Kota, his steadfast Shiba Inu, sat alert. The dog's dark eyes, keen and perceptive, scanned the chaotic landscape for any hint of movement, any sign that danger lurked just beyond the haze. Ever since the Time Rapture, when reality itself had splintered and timelines had intermingled, the world had become a shattered reflection of its former self.

Once-proud skyscrapers now jutted from the earth like broken teeth, and streets that had once thrummed with life were now empty corridors of memory. Ryo remembered the time before—when laughter and the hum of daily life filled every corner of the city—but that had long since vanished, leaving only remnants of a life now lost. Ryo exhaled slowly.

"Stay close, Kota," he murmured, his voice barely audible. The dog tilted his head as if in understanding before returning his focus to the world beyond. Every step forward was a step into uncertainty, and every sound—a creak, a distant crash—could mean either salvation or danger. He rose from his hiding spot and began to move cautiously along a narrow alley, his boots crunching over shattered glass and rubble.

The air was thick with the acrid smell of burning metal and rotting concrete—a constant reminder of the devastation wrought by time itself. The once-gleaming signs of commerce and life were now faded, their messages erased by years of neglect and chaos. As he advanced, Ryo's mind wandered to memories of the past: the day he brought Kota home, the first time the dog had barked in warning as time anomalies flickered at the edge of his vision, and the many nights he had spent alone, haunted by visions of what had been and what might have been.

Kota had become his anchor, his constant in a world where nothing else made sense. Ryo paused at the mouth of an abandoned storefront. The glass was shattered, and the interior was a jumble of overturned shelves, scattered debris, and graffiti marking the walls in desperate strokes of colour.

He could almost hear the distant echoes of the bustle of a busy day—and for a moment, the memories of a lost era washed over him. But those were just ghosts, remnants of a time when hope was not yet a luxury in a fractured world. A sudden rustle to his right snapped Ryo back to the present. He pressed himself against the wall and listened intently. Kota's ears pricked up, and he let out a low, steady growl. Ryo's hand went to his pipe as he peered around the edge of the doorway.

A pair of gloved hands rifled through a pile of discarded newspapers. His pulse quickened—another scavenger, perhaps, searching for food or salvage in the ruins.

Without hesitation, Ryo stepped out and spoke in a hushed, commanding tone,

"Hey! What are you doing?!" The scavenger jumped, dropping the papers as he scrambled backwards, eyes wide with fear. Ryo didn't wait for a response. He advanced slowly, weapon at the ready. Kota barked sharply, a warning that resonated deep within the confined space.

The scavenger, realizing his precarious position, mumbled apologies and backed away, disappearing into the labyrinth of the decaying city. Ryo exhaled deeply, lowering his guard, but never fully relaxing. Every encounter was a reminder that in this shattered world, trust was as scarce as clean water. Stepping back into the open, Ryo continued down the alley until he reached a wide street where the rubble of collapsed buildings lay scattered like the remnants of a forgotten war. Here, the effects of the Time Rapture were most evident.

The very air seemed to shimmer and waver, as if reality were on the verge of dissolving into a thousand broken fragments. Kota trotted ahead, sniffing at the ground with renewed purpose.

Ryo followed, his eyes scanning the horizon. Beyond the immediate wreckage, a cityscape unfolded—a series of jagged silhouettes, half-destroyed towers, and flickering neon signs that still glowed faintly despite years of neglect. The skyline was a constant reminder of the world that once was, a time when the city was alive with ambition and light. Yet, amidst the ruins, there were signs of resilience. A small garden had taken root in the crack of a concrete slab, green and vibrant against the dull greys of decay. Ryo paused to admire it—a tiny testament to nature's ability to reclaim and heal, even in the bleakest of circumstances.

"See that, Kota?" he said softly, crouching down to inspect the garden.

"Even in the darkest places, life finds a way."

Kota sniffed at a bright green leaf, as if in agreement. As the day wore on, the temperature began to drop. Shadows lengthened, and a chill seeped into the bones of the ruined city. Ryo knew that nightfall brought its own set of perils— time anomalies became more frequent, and unseen dangers crept through the darkened streets. Reluctantly, he decided it was time to find shelter. They made their way toward an old, abandoned building on the outskirts of the city— a structure that had once served as a community centre. Its exterior was pockmarked with bullet holes and covered in layers of peeling paint, but it still stood defiantly against the passage of time. Ryo pushed open the heavy, rusted door and stepped inside. The interior was dim and musty, filled with the soft groans of settling debris. Broken chairs and tables were strewn about, and a large stained-glass window, its colours dulled by years of neglect, cast fractured patterns on the floor.

"This will do for tonight," Ryo said, setting down his bag and carefully placing Kota near a spot where a crumbling wall offered some sign of protection. He cleared a small area, gathering any salvageable items that might help keep them warm through the night—a few old blankets, a couple of unlit candles, and a worn thermos of water. He built a small fire in a metal basin he found near the entrance, coaxing flames to life with dry wood and paper.

The light and warmth were feeble but comforting against the encroaching darkness. As Ryo sat by the fire, his eyes wandered over the battered remnants of the building. Faded photographs, torn posters, and scattered trinkets whispered secrets of happier times. Now, all that remained were memories, and even those seemed to be slipping away with each passing day. The sound of the wind outside carried faint echoes of voices—whispers of a past that refused to fade completely, or perhaps the lingering echoes of the Time Rapture itself.

Ryo couldn't tell. His thoughts drifted to the endless questions that haunted him: How had the world come to this? Could time ever be mended, or was it destined to remain fractured, a perpetual reminder of humanity's hubris? Kota shifted near him, nudging Ryo's hand with his warm muzzle, drawing him back to the present.

The dog's loyalty was the one constant in a world of shifting realities and uncertain futures. Ryo stroked his fur, feeling a bittersweet mix of gratitude and sorrow. In Kota's eyes, he saw the strength to endure, the will to survive, and perhaps, a glimmer of hope for redemption.

Outside, the temperature continued to drop, and Ryo wrapped himself in an old, threadbare coat. He kept one eye on the door, ever vigilant, knowing that in this new world, danger could come from any direction. Time itself was unstable here; the past and future bled into the present, and every creak of the building, every gust of wind, might be the sign of something unforeseen. As the night deepened, Ryo tried to rest, but sleep came in fitful, broken intervals.

In the silence, he could hear the soft, rhythmic beating of his own heart, the occasional shiver of the building settling, and the steady, comforting presence of Kota breathing quietly at his side. His mind churned with memories—of lost friends and family, of a world that once thrived, of moments that now existed only in fragments.

In the darkness, Ryo resolved to seek answers. Tomorrow, he would venture out further into the city, searching for clues hidden among the ruins. He would question the few survivors he encountered, scour abandoned libraries and forgotten archives, and piece together the shattered remnants of a history that might one day guide him to redemption—or at least, to understanding. Before long, however, even the most determined souls must rest.

Ryo finally allowed himself to drift into a light sleep, his dreams filled with fleeting images: bright, fragmented visions of a world bathed in sunlight and brimming with life, intermingled with dark flashes of chaos and despair.

In these dreams, Kota ran freely across green fields that seemed to exist only in memory—a place where time was whole again, unburdened by the fractures that now marred every moment. Morning came gradually, the first pale light creeping over the horizon and filtering through the cracks in the building's walls. Ryo awoke to the sound of birds—if they could still be called birds in this broken world—and the soft, persistent patter of Kota's paws as the dog moved around, stretching and yawning.

The fire had long since dwindled to a few embers, and the chill of the early day had begun to seep into his bones. Ryo rose slowly, careful not to disturb the fragile quiet of the morning. He took one last lingering look at the memories of the night before, then gathered his few belongings. Outside, the city was already stirring with the quiet determination of survivors. A thin layer of dew coated the ruins, and the once-glaring neon lights were now replaced by the subtle, natural glow of dawn. As he stepped out into the open, Ryo felt both the weight of loss and the stirring of hope. The shattered world was unforgiving, a constant reminder of the calamity that had undone the tapestry of time. Yet within its broken beauty, there was a spark—a stubborn, resilient spark that told him that even in the midst of devastation, life could endure.

With Kota trotting faithfully by his side, Ryo began his day. Every step along the cracked pavement, every whispered wind carrying the voices of forgotten times, urged him forward into the unknown. The journey was long, and the path uncertain, but as long as he had Kota and the fragile hope that the world could be mended,

Ryo knew he would keep moving. The past was lost, the future uncertain, but in the present, amid the ruins of the shattered world, life still held meaning. As he pressed on, Ryo carried that sense of mystery with him—a subtle reminder that even in a world torn apart by time, there remained forces whose influence was yet to be fully understood.

It was this quiet, unspoken promise that bolstered his resolve and hinted at a destiny that extended far beyond the immediate struggles of survival. For now, survival was enough. And with each new day, as the light grew a little stronger and the shadows retreated just a bit further, Ryo took solace in the simple fact that even a broken world could, in time, begin to heal.

Chapter 2: Crumbling Echoes

The ruined cityscape stretched before Ryo like an endless canvas of sorrow and shattered dreams. With each step along the cracked pavement, memories of the old world—once vibrant, now ghostly—seeped into his thoughts.

The world after the Time Rapture was not simply a place of desolation; it was a labyrinth of fractured time, where past and future mingled in strange, inexplicable ways. Ryo had learned long ago that survival meant more than simply avoiding the physical dangers lurking in the debris of civilization. It also meant confronting the uncanny phenomena that occurred in the spaces between moments.

Today, as the afternoon light fought its way through thick dust and an ashen sky, Ryo sensed that something unusual was about to happen. Kota, his loyal Shiba Inu, padded beside him with his usual alertness—ears pricked, nose twitching, and eyes scanning for any anomaly that might disturb the fragile order of his world. They walked along a street once lined with bustling shops and vibrant neon signs.

Now, the storefronts were empty husks, their windows shattered and their interiors darkened by neglect. The wind carried whispers of a time long past, almost as if the very bricks and mortar of the buildings were trying to speak. Ryo paused in front of one such storefront—a faded

sign barely readable on a crumbling elevation—
and let his gaze wander over the layers of decay.
Every crack, every patch of graffiti, was a
reminder that the world he once knew had
splintered into a thousand fragments.

"Kota," Ryo murmured softly,

"this isn't just ruins. There's something…
different here."

At his words, the dog's ears twitched, and he
stepped ahead, following a scent only he could
detect. Ryo quickened his pace, following his
companion through the maze of shattered
concrete and rusting metal. In the distance, a
faint, pulsing glow caught his eye—a light that
seemed too steady and deliberate to be a mere
trick of the sun. Intrigued and wary, Ryo urged
Kota onward, heading toward the source. They
rounded a corner where a collapsed overhang
lay like a broken roof across the street. Beneath
it, amidst the piles of debris and discarded
belongings, lay something that immediately
made Ryo stop in his tracks: a shard of crystal, no
larger than the palm of his hand, emanating a
soft blue light. The shard was embedded in a
shallow pit, half-buried in dust and rubble, yet its
glow pulsed with an almost hypnotic rhythm.

Ryo knelt down and reached out a cautious
hand. As his fingers brushed the cool, smooth
surface of the shard, a shiver ran through him.

In that instant, the world around him seemed to slow. The distant hum of the city's decay faded into silence, replaced by a deep, resonant vibration that seemed to come from the very core of the shard. For a moment, time itself appeared to hesitate, as if paying homage to the mysterious object. Kota circled the shard, his nose twitching as he sniffed at it.

Then, with a sudden, almost imperceptible whine, the dog sat down and fixed his gaze upon it, his dark eyes reflecting the blue glow. Ryo felt an odd mixture of awe and trepidation. He had heard the old legends from scattered survivors about these "Time Shards" – remnants of the catastrophic event that splintered time.

They were said to hold echoes of the past, glimpses into memories that were lost to the ages. But until now, he had never encountered one so clearly. Ryo carefully picked up the shard. In his hand, it pulsed more strongly, and he could almost feel its energy vibrating against his skin. As he held it, fleeting images began to surface—a montage of scenes that flashed past like fragments of broken memories.

He saw a smiling child playing in a sunlit park, strangers in a bustling market, and even a glimpse of himself from long ago, full of hope and unburdened by loss. The images were disjointed and fleeting, yet they carried an undeniable weight of significance.

"Do you see it, Kota?" Ryo whispered, his voice trembling with a mixture of wonder and sorrow.

The dog remained silent, his eyes locked onto the shimmering shard as if he too were absorbing its secrets. For several long moments, Ryo sat on the cold, dusty ground, lost in the cascade of images. The shard's glow began to subside and flow, and as it did, the visions shifted.

Now, he saw scenes of chaos—a city in flames, crowds of panicked people, and moments of time colliding in a disorienting spectacle. It was as if the shard was showing him the essence of the Time Rapture itself—the moment when time had fractured and the world had been forever altered.

Ryo's hand tightened around the shard as he fought to regain control of his racing thoughts. He knew that such relics were dangerous; they could easily overwhelm an unprepared mind with the weight of what once was. But he also sensed that this shard held answers, answers about the fate of the world or about the mysterious forces at work. He rose slowly, taking one last lingering look at the glowing fragment before standing.

Reluctantly, Ryo slipped the shard into the inner pocket of his worn jacket, deciding that it was best kept close until he could understand its true nature. Kota trotted up beside him, his gaze steady and reassuring.

"We need to move," Ryo said, pushing himself off the cold ground.

"There's no telling what else might be here." With Kota by his side and the shard safely stowed away, Ryo resumed his journey through the broken streets. Here, the effects of the Time Rapture were most evident.

The very air shimmered with distortions, and every so often, Ryo would catch a glimpse of figures that seemed not quite solid—fleeting shadows that vanished as quickly as they appeared. At one point, as they moved through a particularly narrow alley, Ryo heard the sound of voices—a soft, indistinct murmur that seemed to come from all around him. He stopped in his tracks and listened.

The voices were layered, overlapping in a disconcerting harmony of past and present. For a moment, he could almost discern fragments of conversation—a snippet of laughs, a whisper of sorrow—but the meaning was lost in the jumble of sounds.

"Maybe the shard is doing that," he muttered, glancing at Kota. The dog only tilted his head, as if acknowledging the unspoken possibility that the shard's presence might be influencing the distortions in time. Ryo pressed on, his mind heavy with questions and the weight of his recent visions. Every building, every shattered remnant of the old world, seemed to speak to him of both loss and possibility.

The visions from the shard reminded him that time was not just a linear progression, but a tapestry of moments—some of them beautiful, others tragic—woven together by forces he could scarcely comprehend. As the afternoon waned, the sun began its slow descent behind the horizon, casting the ruins in long, distorted shadows. Ryo and Kota found themselves at the edge of a once-bustling marketplace. Now, the market was a silent graveyard of abandoned stalls and overturned carts.

A thick layer of dust covered everything, and the only sound was the soft scuffle of Kota's paws on the cracked pavement. In the centre of the marketplace, a broken fountain stood as a relic of better times. Its water long since evaporated, the stone basin was overgrown with moss and lichen.

Ryo walked up to it and knelt, running his fingers over the intricate carvings that decorated its edge. Each symbol seemed to tell a story—a story of hope, of community, of lives once intertwined. For a moment, he allowed himself to remember, to imagine the conversations that once echoed here and the warmth of human connection. But then, as quickly as the memory came, it faded. The world around him was harsh and unyielding now. With a sigh, Ryo rose and resumed his journey. He needed shelter soon; nightfall in the fractured city was dangerous, and the distortions only grew more erratic as darkness fell. Navigating through winding alleys and past crumbling structures, Ryo finally reached a broken-down building that had once served as a Post Office.

Its elevation was scarred with time, and the heavy door creaked ominously as he pushed it open. Inside, the vast space was filled with the remnants of a bygone era: dusty benches, scattered books, and faded murals that depicted scenes of unity and hope.

Despite the decay, there was a certain solemn beauty to the place—a silent testament to what had once been. Ryo found a relatively secure corner near a broken wall and spread out a threadbare blanket he'd scavenged from a pile of old clothes. Kota, ever loyal, curled up beside him. Before settling down, Ryo took one last look at the shard hidden safely in his pocket.

He knew that this object was no mere relic; it was a key—a piece of the puzzle that might one day explain the unfathomable events that had torn the world apart. As dusk gave way to night, the building fell silent except for the occasional creak of settling debris. Ryo sat in the dim light of a salvaged lantern, its weak flame casting dancing shadows on the cracked walls. In the quiet, his mind replayed the visions the shard had shown him. Faces and places he barely recognized drifted through his thoughts, mingling with the steady rhythm of his heartbeat.

He wondered about the nature of time—how it could be broken, reassembled, and yet remain so elusive. Sleep did not come easily that night. Ryo lay awake, listening to the wind outside and the soft, rhythmic breathing of Kota. He knew that with each passing day, the stakes grew higher. The shard's visions were both a promise and a threat—promising a glimpse of a world that might be restored, yet warning of the sacrifices that such restoration might require.

Morning came slowly, the first pale light seeping through the broken windows. Ryo rose, careful not to disturb Kota, who had been sleeping soundly by his side. The chill in the air reminded him that time was a relentless force, indifferent to the frailties of those who lived within its grasp. Today, he decided, he would seek out more clues about the mysterious shard.

Perhaps there were others who had encountered similar phenomena, or perhaps ancient records lay hidden among the ruins, waiting to divulge the secrets of the Time Rapture. Stepping out into the uncertain light of dawn, Ryo felt a renewed determination. The city, despite its shattered state, was alive with whispers of the past and promises of the future.

Every cracked wall, every flickering light, was a testament to resilience in the face of overwhelming loss. And in his pocket, the shard pulsed softly—a reminder that even in a world torn apart by chaos, fragments of truth could still be found. Kota trotted alongside him as Ryo retraced his steps through the labyrinthine streets. They moved with a silent urgency, wary of the dangers that lurked in the intersections of fractured time.

The visions from the shard lingered in his mind, and he couldn't help but wonder: were those glimpses mere memories of what once was, or hints of what could be if time were somehow mended? As the day wore on, Ryo encountered other survivors—haggard figures who spoke in hushed tones about "the cracks" and "the voices of time."

Their stories were fragmented, much like the world they inhabited, yet they all pointed to one inescapable truth: the Time Rapture was not an isolated disaster, but a fundamental rupture in the fabric of existence. And within that rupture lay the potential for both unimaginable destruction and a chance at renewal. By late afternoon, Ryo reached the outskirts of the city—a desolate district where nature had begun its slow reclamation.

Overgrown vines snaked over ruined walls and wildflowers pushed through cracks in the concrete. Here, in this liminal space between urban decay and wild resurgence, Ryo paused to catch his breath. He knelt down, pulling the shard from his pocket once more. In the soft, dying light, the crystal pulsed steadily, as if resonating with the heartbeat of the earth itself.

For a long moment, he simply held it, letting the cool energy seep into his skin. The visions came back in waves—a montage of voices, images, and emotions that blurred the lines between dream and reality. He saw faces of loved ones lost, fleeting glimpses of a future unburdened by the chaos of fractured time, and even a vision of Kota as a younger, more vibrant creature bounding through a sunlit field.

Each vision was a shard of its own, a tiny sliver of possibility amidst the overwhelming darkness. Ryo's eyes narrowed as a thought crystallized in his mind. If these shards were echoes of the past and signals of the future, then perhaps they were clues—a way to piece together the mystery of the Time Rapture. Determined to learn more, he resolved to seek out any information he could find. There were rumours of old archives hidden in the depths of ruined libraries, of survivors who had managed to salvage books and records from the collapse. Perhaps among these relics lay the answers to the questions that now plagued him.

Night fell quickly, and with it came a deep, oppressive silence that blanketed the ruins. Ryo found shelter in a small, abandoned office on the edge of the district—a temporary refuge from the perils of the night.

For every moment of despair, there was a spark of possibility—if only one had the courage to seek it out. As the embers of a makeshift fire flickered in the darkness, Ryo stared at the shard one last time before sleep claimed him. In its gentle, pulsing glow, he saw not only reflections of what once was, but also the promise of what might be—a future waiting patiently on the other side of time's fractured mirror.

Chapter 3: Chasing the Lost

The city's outskirts were a wasteland of broken dreams and crumbling concrete—a place where time itself had left scars that no one could heal. Ryo and Kota moved carefully through the maze of ruined streets and shattered architecture, every step measured and every sound scrutinized. After days of traveling through unstable landscapes and dodging time distortions, their path led them to a derelict industrial quarter.

Here, the remnants of once-thriving factories and warehouses bore silent testimony to a world that had long since collapsed into chaos. Ryo's eyes scanned the horizon as he adjusted the strap on his battered backpack. He could see the distant glimmer of anomalies—iridescent rifts that pulsed like the heartbeat of a dying world.

Yet amid the desolation, a new presence loomed. Shadows moved with predatory precision, and murmurs of activity broke the heavy silence. His instincts told him that they were not alone. Kota trotted at his side, every muscle alert, every ear pricked forward. The loyal Shiba Inu had become Ryo's compass in this fractured reality, sensing dangers even before they emerged.

Today, Kota's low growl and tense posture warned of imminent peril. Ryo quickened his pace, turning into a narrow alley framed by collapsed brick walls and twisted metal. At the far end of the alley, a faint sound of clashing metal and hushed voices reached his ears. Ryo pressed himself against the wall and peered around the corner. There, in a small open space littered with debris and discarded remnants of machinery, a group of figures were gathered.

Their postures were predatory, and their movements calculated—a stark contrast to the mindless scavenging Ryo had witnessed before. They were the Rift Hunters. Dressed in mismatched armour forged from scrap metal, leather, and faded uniforms, these men and women had the air of hardened survivors who had long since learned that the fractured world rewarded ruthlessness.

Their eyes, cold and calculating, scanned the environment as one of them stepped forward, his voice low and menacing.

"Scavengers—always wandering in search of a scrap of hope," he sneered.

"But hope isn't for sale."

Ryo's heart pounded as he recognized the leader's tone. These were not ordinary desperate souls; they were predators, exploiting the chaos for power and profit. Ryo's grip on his makeshift spear tightened. He exchanged a look with Kota—a silent acknowledgment that they were in trouble.

The leader's eyes swept the area until they landed on a shadow moving beyond the debris.

"There!" he shouted, and in that instant, the group sprang into action. Their shouts echoed through the alley as they surged forward, weapons drawn—a jagged blade in one hand, a crude club in another, and even a salvaged rifle slung over a shoulder. Ryo bolted from his hiding place, Kota darting alongside him as the Hunters advanced.

The narrow corridor turned into a gauntlet of chaos as the scavengers pursued with relentless determination. Ryo's pulse thundered in his ears as he sprinted along the alley, weaving between collapsed columns and piles of rubble. The clamour of footsteps and the clash of improvised weapons filled the air.

Ryo glanced back occasionally to see the silhouettes of the Rift Hunters gaining ground. His mind raced—this was not a chance encounter; these people had been tracking him. Their motives were as murky as the distortions that plagued this broken world. A sharp cry rang out as one of the Hunters lunged at him from the side. Ryo barely had time to raise his spear, the metal pipe glinting in the weak light, and drive it forward. The attacker stumbled, a pained groan escaping his lips as he fell against the wall. But the danger was far from over.

Kota, ever vigilant, intercepted another assailant. With a flash of ferocity unexpected for his size, the Shiba leaped and bit down hard on the arm of a Hunter attempting to grab Ryo. The man's yell of pain echoed off the crumbling walls, and for a brief moment, chaos halted as the group's focus shifted. Ryo seized the opening.

"Run, Kota!" he shouted, pushing forward with every ounce of strength. Kota barked in response, the sound a mixture of defiance and determination. Together, they sprinted down a side street, the pounding of their feet and the roar of distant conflict spurring them onward. The alley gave way to a wider boulevard strewn.

The sky above was a bruised canvas, the late afternoon sun barely piercing the ever-present haze. Ryo's mind was a whirlwind of adrenaline and fear. Every turn, every shadow, could hide another enemy. The Rift Hunters were not easily deterred—they were relentless, and they knew the wasteland well.

As they ran, Ryo caught sight of a flicker—a group of Hunters, their faces masked in scavenged cloth and their eyes gleaming with malice, blocking the path ahead. There was no way around them; Ryo's options were running thin. With a grim determination, he braced himself for confrontation.

"Stay behind me, Kota," he said, his voice

steady despite the turmoil inside. He squared his shoulders and stepped forward to meet the threat head-on. The Hunters halted their advance, their leader emerging once more with a cold, calculated smile.

"You have skill," the leader remarked, his tone dripping with both sarcasm and respect.

"But you're on our turf now. We can offer you sanctuary—for a price." Ryo's eyes narrowed.

"I'm not for sale." A bitter laugh escaped the leader.

"Oh, you misunderstand. It's not you we want—it's what you might bring us. That dog of yours… he's something special. We know he's connected to the anomalies, to the very essence of time. Hand him over, and perhaps we can spare you further trouble."

Ryo's blood boiled. He tightened his grip on his spear, his gaze never leaving the leader's.

"Leave my dog alone!" The Hunter's smile faded into a sneer.

"We are the Rift Hunters. We thrive in the broken spaces where time fractures and power is born from chaos. You and your dog are nothing but scraps in a world we can shape as we please." With a shout, the confrontation erupted into violence. Ryo charged forward, dodging a swing from a crude club while lunging at another assailant. Metal clanged against metal as Ryo's spear met the Hunter's blade in a shower of sparks. The narrow boulevard transformed into a battleground—shouts, clashes, and the sound of feet pounding against shattered concrete filled the air. Kota fought with a ferocity born of survival. He leapt at a Hunter attempting to snatch Ryo's bag, his teeth sinking into fabric and skin alike. The scuffle was swift and brutal; in the chaos, several Hunters fell, their cries swallowed by the din of battle.

Despite his determination, Ryo knew that brute force alone would not save them. The Rift Hunters were numerous, and their experience in the wasteland gave them an edge. He fought desperately, his eyes never leaving Kota as he navigated the scuffle. Every time he glanced at his loyal companion, Ryo was reminded that his survival depended not just on his own strength, but on the bond they shared. After what felt like an eternity, the tide of the battle began to shift.

More Hunters arrived from the depths of the boulevard, their voices merging into a relentless chorus of threats. Ryo's muscles burned with exertion, and his breath came in ragged gasps. In the midst of the encounter, the leader of the Hunters called out,

"Enough! You have made your point." A heavy silence fell for a heartbeat as the scattered combatants hesitated. The leader's voice, cold and commanding, cut through the chaos:

"We can't afford this chase. We need not kill you both, but you must understand—the wasteland does not tolerate weakness."

With that, the remaining Hunters began to retreat, melting back into the shadows from where they came. Ryo, his body trembling from exhaustion and adrenaline, leaned against a wall to catch his breath. Kota circled him warily, still on high alert despite the dispersal of the attackers.

"Not bad," Ryo murmured, though his voice was strained.

"You fought well, boy." He reached down to ruffle Kota's fur, gratitude and sorrow mingling in his tired eyes. They had escaped this confrontation, but the encounter left a bitter taste. The words of the Hunters echoed in his mind—their desire to exploit Kota's strange connection to the anomalies, to harness the power of fractured time for their own ends. As the echoes of battle faded, Ryo knew that this encounter was only the beginning.

The Rift Hunters were more than mere scavengers; they were opportunists who thrived on the chaos, and they would continue to pursue them as long as there was any hint of value in the broken world. His mind raced with possibilities—and dangers. Who else might be after Kota?

What secrets lay hidden within his loyal companion, whose very presence seemed to command the fractured winds of time? With the confrontation behind him, Ryo and Kota resumed their journey through the ruined industrial quarter. The scars of the battle were evident: fresh marks on the walls where claws and blades had struck, and the metallic tang of blood mingling with the dusty air. Yet for Ryo, every bruise and every scar served as a reminder that survival was the only option. The remainder of the day passed in a tense, watchful silence.

Ryo kept a constant eye on the darkened alleys and open spaces, every sound a potential warning of new danger. Kota, ever the vigilant guardian, never strayed far from his side. Their bond was their strength—a silent promise that they would protect each other at all costs. As dusk approached, the sky turned a deep, foreboding red. Shadows lengthened, and the fractured city seemed to hold its breath in anticipation of nightfall. Ryo knew that darkness in the wasteland was more than just a lack of light—it was a time when the anomalies grew stronger, and threats lurked unseen.

Finding a relatively secure nook in a collapsed warehouse, Ryo set about making a temporary camp. He scavenged what little firewood he could find among the rubble and managed to kindle a small, flickering flame in a rusted metal basin. The fire's light danced across the warped walls, offering a fragile barrier against the encroaching gloom.

Sitting by the fire, Ryo allowed himself a moment to reflect on the day's harrowing events. The encounter with the Rift Hunters, their ruthless ambition—to capture and exploit anomalies, to control the very flow of time—was a threat that loomed as large as the broken skyline. Kota lay near Ryo's feet, his breathing steady but his eyes ever watchful. Ryo patted his head gently, his mind churning with questions.

Why were these people so obsessed with Kota? What did they see in the dog that made him worth risking lives for? Though Ryo had always sensed that Kota was more than just a companion, the day's events had cemented a cold certainty: in a world torn apart by the Time Rapture, even the smallest spark of power could ignite a firestorm of greed and cruelty.

The night deepened, and with it came an oppressive silence that seemed to press against the walls of their makeshift shelter. Ryo's thoughts turned to the future—a future where the scars of today might one day heal, or where every choice could lead to further ruin. The shard he'd found earlier, the visions it had shown him, and the relentless pursuit of the Rift Hunters—all were pieces of a puzzle that he intended to solve, no matter how high the cost. In the quiet moments before sleep, Ryo whispered to Kota,

"We'll get through this, boy. I promise. We'll find the answers we need and protect what matters most."

Kota responded with a soft, reassuring whine—a sound that carried both loyalty and a mysterious, unspoken understanding.

Chapter 4: Whispered Signs

The late afternoon light filtered weakly through a sky shrouded in dust, casting a faint glow over the remnants of what once was a bustling overpass. Now, only jagged slabs of concrete and twisted metal remained, extending out like broken bones against the horizon. Ryo and Kota moved cautiously among the rubble, their footsteps muffled by the soft layer of ash that covered the ground. Ryo's heart pounded as he scanned the area. Every shattered fragment, every rusted beam, seemed to whisper echoes of a world lost to time.

He had learned never to let his guard down— not in this fractured existence where danger lurked in every shadow, and time itself was an unruly force. Beside him, Kota's ears were perked and his eyes alert. The Shiba Inu's gaze darted from one darkened wall to another, as if reading secrets hidden in the debris.

For Ryo, Kota had become more than a companion; he was a beacon in this chaotic landscape, a steady presence in a world where nothing was certain. They had chosen this place—beneath the collapsed overpass—as a temporary refuge from the dangers that roamed the ruined streets. The overpass had once carried thousands of vehicles, its arches a testament to human ambition. Now, its remnants offered scant shelter, but they were better than being exposed in the open wasteland. Ryo led Kota beneath a large, overhanging concrete slab.

He set down his bag carefully and moved to inspect the area for any signs of disturbance. The wind stirred slowly, carrying with it faint sounds that might have been mistaken for voices or perhaps the groans of a structure settling into oblivion. A moment of uneasy quiet enveloped them. Suddenly, a soft sound—a gentle rustle— echoed from further inside the ruins. Ryo's hand instinctively went to the knife at his belt, and Kota immediately tensed beside him. From the shadowed recess of the collapsed structure, a figure emerged.

At first, it was only a silhouette, barely visible against the twilight. The figure moved with a measured grace that belied the chaos surrounding them. As they drew closer, Ryo could see that it was a woman, dressed in a dark, worn cloak that blended into the rubble.

Her face was partially hidden by a hood, but when she finally stepped into a shaft of fading light, her eyes—an intense, almost unnerving golden hue—met his. For a long, suspended moment, neither spoke. The silence was punctuated only by the soft sound of the wind shifting through the broken concrete. Ryo's muscles tensed, every instinct warning him that this stranger was not there by chance.

Then, in a voice that was both gentle and firm, she spoke:

"Trust the dog when the time comes." Her words, simple yet loaded with implication, sent a shiver down Ryo's spine. He blinked, uncertain whether he had heard correctly. Kota, however, remained completely still, fixated on the woman as if understanding her message.

"Who are you?" Ryo demanded, his tone cautious but edged with authority. The woman lowered her hood slowly, revealing delicate features framed by streaks of dark hair. Her eyes, still burning with that mysterious light, studied him for a moment.

"I am Kaori," she replied softly.

"I've been waiting for you." Ryo's grip on his knife did not loosen, though he felt a strange pull in his gut—a mix of apprehension and an inexplicable sense of destiny.

"Waiting for me?" he asked, glancing at Kota, whose expression was mysterious but calm. Kaori's gaze shifted to the dog, and a small, almost imperceptible smile touched her lips.

"There are things about your companion that you have yet to understand, Ryo." Ryo frowned, taken aback by her familiarity.

"How do you know my name?" he pressed, the question laden with both disbelief and a growing sense of destiny. A small, sad smile played upon her lips as she regarded him with unspoken understanding.

"The winds of time carry many whispers, Ryo," she murmured.

"I have listened to them for years, and your name was spoken with such profound longing and hope that it could not be ignored. You are destined for a path that reaches far beyond these ruins." Her words, both enigmatic and stirring, sent a ripple of uncertainty through Ryo's heart.

Though her identity remained shrouded in mystery, the fact that she knew him felt like both a blessing and a burden. It was a silent promise that the threads of fate were already weaving his future—a future where the shattered fragments of time might yet be mended. Ryo's gaze softened as he absorbed her words, and despite his lingering wariness, a part of him welcomed the guidance. The mysterious figure's presence, her knowledge of his very name, hinted at a destiny larger than his own suffering—a promise that even in the darkest of times, there were forces at work determined to restore balance. Kaori continued to speak about the Shiba Inu.

"Kota is not simply a loyal pet. He is intertwined with the very fabric of time. And now, the fractured world is calling out for change." Ryo's mind raced. He had always sensed that Kota was special—more than just a survivor in this broken world—but the idea that the dog might be linked to the mysteries of time was both awe-inspiring and terrifying.

"What do you mean?" he pressed, lowering his weapon slightly but never fully trusting her. Kaori stepped closer, her presence both soothing and unnerving.

"The rifts, the distortions you see—they are not random. They are the echoes of a grand design gone awry. When the Time Rapture shattered reality, it left behind fragments—pieces of a greater whole. And among those fragments, one stands out: the Timekeeper's Heart. That, Ryo, is what Kota is. He resonates with the energy of time itself." Ryo frowned, trying to reconcile her words with the reality he had lived every day since the collapse.

"I don't understand. You're saying my dog… is a key? A beacon? Some sort of living timepiece?" Kaori nodded slowly.

"Not just a timepiece—a guardian of the temporal flow. His very being stabilizes the chaos, even if he is unaware of it. And the disturbances you see—the rifts that warp our reality—are drawn to him. They seek him out, as if he holds the key to mending what has been broken." The idea was staggering. Ryo had spent countless days fighting off scavengers and navigating the treacherous streets, and all the while, Kota had been his constant, his comfort. But to think that this faithful companion might be linked to the very nature of time was almost too fantastical to believe. Before Ryo could voice his doubts, a distant rumble interrupted their conversation—a deep, resonant sound that seemed to emanate from beneath the overpass itself. The ground trembled slightly, and a fine layer of dust began to settle once more. Kaori's eyes darkened for a moment, and she stepped back as if bracing herself.

"Time is shifting again," she said quietly.

"There is instability in the fractures. The convergence draws near, and soon, forces beyond your control will seek to exploit what you possess."

Ryo exchanged a worried glance with Kota, who now sniffed the air with heightened urgency. The tremors had grown slightly stronger, and the very atmosphere seemed charged with an unseen energy.

"Who—who is coming?" Ryo asked, his voice a hushed whisper. Kaori's gaze hardened, and she took a measured breath.

"The Time Weavers are protectors, and others more dangerous still lurk in the shadows, the Rift Hunters. They hunger for the power that flows within the Timekeeper's Heart. If they capture Kota, they will use him to bend time to their will, regardless of the cost." Ryo's fists clenched.

"I won't let that happen. You speak of things beyond my understanding, but I know one thing—I won't sacrifice Kota. He's been with me through everything." Kaori stepped forward again, her eyes softening as she regarded him.

"I do not ask you to make a choice lightly, Ryo. The path before you is treacherous, and every moment brings you closer to a decision that will shape the fate of this fractured world. But heed my words: when the time comes, trust the bond you share with Kota. It is more powerful than you realize." Silence fell between them as the tremors subsided, leaving only the distant rumble of shifting earth. Ryo's mind whirled with conflicting emotions—suspicion, hope, and a dawning realization that perhaps fate had led him to this moment.

"Why are you telling me all of this?" he asked.

"What do you want?" Kaori's expression remained unreadable.

"I have seen visions—echoes of what might be if the threads of time are not mended. I cannot change what has already happened, but I can guide you. The choices you make now will echo across all timelines, and the future depends on your willingness to act." A heavy pause stretched between them, punctuated only by the soft murmur of the wind through broken metal and the distant call of a lone bird. Ryo felt the weight of her words settle deep within him. He looked down at Kota, who sat with an air of quiet dignity despite the uncertainty swirling around them.

"And if I refuse?" he asked, his voice barely more than a whisper. Kaori's eyes gleamed with both sorrow and determination.

"Then the world will continue to unravel, and countless lives will be lost in the chaos. You have a chance—no, a duty—to protect not only what remains of your own world but to preserve the very fabric of time. I cannot force you, Ryo, but know that there is no turning back once the convergence begins."

Ryo's thoughts tumbled over one another. Every instinct told him to dismiss Kaori's words as the ravings of a desperate soul clinging to hope in a shattered world. Yet, there was something about the certainty in her voice—a knowledge that went beyond mere superstition—that made him pause.

He recalled the odd occurrences with Kota: the way the dog's eyes would sometimes glow in the presence of a rift, or how the air around him seemed to shimmer as if touched by an unseen energy. All these small signs, once brushed aside as coincidence, now formed a pattern that he could no longer ignore.

"Tell me, what must I do?" Ryo said slowly, How can I protect Kota—and perhaps, mend this broken time?" Kaori regarded him with an intensity that made him feel both exposed and seen.

"There is a way, but it will require the willingness to embrace the unknown. You must seek the lost knowledge of the old world— hidden in the ruins, in the whispers of survivors, in the relics of the Time Rapture. Only by understanding what shattered time can you hope to restore it." Her words stirred something deep within him—a mixture of determination and dread. Ryo knew that his journey had always been about survival, but now it was taking on a higher purpose, a quest for redemption not only for himself but for the fractured reality that surrounded him.

As twilight deepened, Kaori stepped back into the shifting shadows beneath the overpass.

"I will not remain here, but remember my warning: When the convergence comes, when the forces that seek to exploit Kota grow too strong, trust the bond you share with him. That bond is the key to your survival—and to the salvation of time itself." Before Ryo could ask another question, she melted away into the darkness, leaving him alone beneath the collapsed concrete.

The wind sighed through the gaps in the structure, as if carrying her final words with it. Ryo sank to his knees, clutching his head as he tried to process the torrent of revelations. Kota padded over and nuzzled his hand, a gentle reminder that amidst the chaos, he was not alone. Slowly, Ryo drew a shaky breath and looked into the dog's steadfast eyes.

"We have work to do, boy," he murmured, voice heavy with resolve.

"I don't know what lies ahead, but I promise I'll protect you—no matter the cost."

The overpass loomed above them like a monument to a lost era, its broken arches a silent witness to the promise that Ryo had just made.

The fractured sky overhead pulsed with the faint glow of approaching night, and somewhere in the distance, the rumble of unseen forces grew louder—a signal of the convergence that Kaori had foretold. As darkness fell, Ryo gathered his few belongings and helped Kota to his feet.

Together, they stepped away from the shelter of the collapsed overpass, their path lit only by the trembling light of distant fires and the occasional flash of a time rift that tore momentarily at the fabric of reality. Every step was a step into the unknown—a journey that would test their courage, reshape their destinies, and challenge the very nature of time.

For in a world where time was broken, the bond between man and his faithful dog was the one constant that could still ignite hope—a spark in the darkness, promising that even the shattered pieces of existence might one day be made whole again. And so, beneath the crumbling arches of the overpass and the fading light of day, Ryo began the next leg of his journey. His heart was heavy with the weight of destiny, yet fierce with determination.

The convergence loomed on the horizon, and with every step, he embraced the uncertainty of the future, guided by the unyielding loyalty of Kota and the cryptic, lingering echo of Kaori's warning.

Chapter 5: Ash Roads

The sky was a bleeding canvas of orange and red as Ryo and Kota emerged from the crumbling urban labyrinth. Behind them, the chaotic echoes of battle with the Rift Hunters still rang in their ears—but ahead lay the vast, unforgiving area known as the Wastes.

Here, the broken remnants of civilization gave way to barren fields of cracked earth, twisted metal, and a silence that felt both endless and oppressive. Ryo's breath came in ragged gasps as he pressed forward along a debris-strewn road. Every footfall on the parched pavement was a reminder of the fragility of life in a world where time had been divided.

Beside him, Kota trotted with unwavering loyalty, ears alert and eyes scanning the horizon. In this place, danger was not always visible; it could lurk in the shimmering heat of a mirage, in the rustle of dried grasses, or in the whisper of a time distortion that twisted reality ever so slightly. They had barely escaped the urban ambush—a savage melee with the Rift Hunters—when Ryo had resolved that staying in the crumbling industrial zones wouldn't be the best solution.

Now, with dusk approaching, they had no choice but to press onward. he Wastes were as unpredictable as they were vast, a no-man's-land where the rules of time and space were no longer guaranteed. As Ryo navigated the debris, memories of past confrontations mingled with the desolation of the present.

He recalled the ferocity of the Hunters' assault, the desperate clanging of metal on concrete, and Kota's brave, ferocious defence. Even now, the sight of his loyal companion—bruised yet unbowed—lent him the strength to continue. Every step forward was not just an act of survival; it was a defiant refusal to succumb to despair. The landscape stretched out in an endless region of broken pavement and scattered relics.

Once, this road had been a major artery connecting the heart of the city to its outskirts. Now it was little more than a scar in the earth—a route over which nature and time had begun to reclaim their domain. In places, wild, untamed vegetation had pushed through the fissures in the concrete, and the cracked ground was patterned with deep lines that looked like the wrinkles of a long-forgotten giant. Ryo's eyes, sharp despite exhaustion, caught a glimmer on the horizon—a wavering shimmer that moved like a heat mirage.

He slowed his pace, squinting against the low sun. For a brief moment, it appeared as if there were a cluster of structures rising from the flatlands—a ghost village, perhaps, or an oasis in the desert of destruction. But as he approached, the vision shifted and dissolved into nothingness, leaving him with only the unsettling knowledge that in the Wastes, reality was as unstable as the memories of what had been.

"Kota, this place... it's like nothing I've ever seen. Everything here feels out of time."

Kota's ears twitched as he sniffed the air, his gaze fixed on something beyond the immediate path. Ryo felt that the dog was sensing disturbances—tiny ripples in the fabric of reality that foretold hidden dangers. With every step, Ryo's thoughts churned: Was this wasteland merely a barren stretch of land, or was it a threshold to something even more unpredictable? They rounded a curve in the road and entered a vast open plain.

The remnants of the urban sprawl receded behind them, replaced by an endless field of cracked, sun-baked earth. Here, the silence was almost absolute, broken only by the distant sound of a loose stone skittering across the ground and the soft whisper of a wind that carried the scent of dust and old regrets.

Ryo paused, crouching down to examine a patch of ground where the earth had split open like a wound. Tiny fissures ran through the cracked soil, and in the centre of one such fracture, he noticed an unusual glint. He knelt closer, brushing aside a thin layer of dust with a calloused hand. Embedded in the earth was a small, metallic fragment that shimmered oddly in the fading light—an echo of technology from before the collapse.

He pocketed it without a word; every artifact was a clue to the past, and every scrap held its own story of a world that once was. As the sun sank lower, the temperature began to drop rapidly. The oppressive heat of the day gave way to a biting chill, and long shadows stretched across the Wastes like dark fingers reaching out to ensnare the unwary.

Ryo quickened his pace, knowing that nightfall in these lands was a perilous time. Time distortions were more frequent after dark, and creatures—both human and otherwise—ventured out under the cloak of darkness. The path soon took them to a ridge overlooking a vast, desolate valley.

From this vantage, Ryo could see the full extent of the Wastes: endless stretches of parched earth punctuated by jagged rock formations and the occasional cluster of withered trees. The horizon was dominated by a fractured sky, its colours swirling in muted shades of purple and grey.

It was here, atop this lonely ridge, that Ryo allowed himself a moment to catch his breath.

"Kota," he said, sitting down on a rock, "we've come a long way today. But I can't shake the feeling that we're not alone out here."

Kota merely sat beside him, head tilted as if listening for distant voices. The silence of the valley was deep, almost unnerving, yet it carried a subtle promise of hidden wonders—a possibility that amidst the broken time, there might be clues to rebuilding a world lost.

After a few moments, Ryo stood and resumed their journey. The valley below beckoned like an uncharted realm, and despite the inherent danger, the hope of finding shelter or answers drove him onward. As they descended the ridge, the landscape transformed again.

The rough, sun-scorched plains gave way to an area where nature had begun to reclaim its hold. Sparse vegetation clung to life in the form of scraggly bushes and resilient grasses, their green hues a stark contrast against the desolation. The descent was treacherous.

Loose gravel and uneven ground forced Ryo to slow his pace, every step a careful negotiation with the unforgiving terrain. Kota led the way confidently, his every move precise and assured. Even in this broken landscape, the dog's intuition shone through—guiding Ryo along paths that were hidden, treacherous, yet somehow promising safety.

After what seemed like hours of cautious travel, the duo reached the edge of a ruined settlement—a ghostly remnant of a once-thriving community now swallowed by the Wastes. Buildings, half-collapsed and overgrown with wild vines, lined a narrow street that wound through the settlement like a forgotten memory.

Here, the air was cooler, and the distortions in time were subtle—a faint shimmer on the horizon, a soft echo of voices that might have once filled the streets with life. Ryo hesitated at the boundary of the settlement. It was not the open wasteland that frightened him, but rather the potential that it held. The stories of survivors said that abandoned towns like these were often haunted—not just by ghosts of the past, but by the restless echoes of time itself.

Yet, the promise of shelter and perhaps even forgotten knowledge was too compelling to ignore.

"We'll take a look," he said to Kota, determination lacing his tone.

"Just a quick search for anything useful, then we move on." The two stepped cautiously into the settlement. Every creak of a broken board, every rustle of wind through shattered windows, set Ryo's nerves on edge. The streets were silent, the only movement the slow dance of dust particles in the faint light.

Ryo kept his senses alert as he scanned doorways and windows, searching for signs of life or salvageable supplies. In one broken building—a former general store—Ryo discovered a trove of relics: faded photographs, half-buried in a pile of newspapers, and a small, rusted safe that might once have held valuables.

He rummaged through the items carefully, selecting a few objects that could be useful or at least serve as clues to the past. Each find was a piece of a puzzle that might one day help him understand the full impact of the Time Rapture. While Ryo was busy searching, Kota ventured further down the street. The dog paused before a crumbling wall and began to bark softly. Ryo called out,

"Kota, come here!"

But the dog was fixated on something hidden in the shadows—a small, almost imperceptible movement. Ryo followed, his hand instinctively reaching for his weapon. In the dim light, he glimpsed a figure slipping away into an alley. Before he could react, the figure vanished. Was it a survivor? A scavenger? Or something else entirely—a remnant of the fractured times?

The encounter left Ryo with more questions than answers. But time was short. The chill of dusk was setting in, and he could feel the weight of unseen eyes watching from the ruins.

Gathering his few finds, he rejoined Kota and led the way out of the settlement. The promise of shelter, however, was bittersweet. The settlement was silent, a ghost of a community, and its emptiness was a stark reminder of the lives lost to the Time Rapture. Back on the open road, the sky darkened rapidly. Night in the Wastes was a realm of its own—full of shifting shadows, sudden time distortions, and dangers unseen in the harsh light of day. Ryo and Kota quickened their pace, their silhouettes merging with the growing darkness as they moved along the cracked pavement. The wind picked up, carrying with it a chill that seeped into Ryo's bones. Every now and then, the air vibrated with an almost musical quality—a low hum that resonated with the pulse of the earth.

Ryo couldn't help but feel that the very fabric of time was alive in the Wastes, whispering secrets and warnings in a language older than humankind. As they trekked on, the road led them to a wide, barren plain bordered by jagged rock formations. The plain was illuminated by the eerie light of a half-hidden moon, and the ground shimmered with frost as the temperature plummeted. Ryo pulled his worn coat tighter around him, his eyes scanning the horizon for any sign of movement. The silence was profound—a silence that felt like it stretched into eternity, broken only by the crunch of their footsteps on the frosty ground. In the midst of this desolation, Ryo's thoughts turned once again to the shard and Kaori's warning. He wondered what fate awaited them and whether the visions he had experienced might someday offer a glimmer of hope—or if they were merely echoes of a world that had been lost forever.

Hours passed, and the landscape gradually softened into a gentle wave of dunes and rocky outcrops. The Wastes, for all its harshness, had moments of unexpected beauty. At one point, Ryo paused on a high ridge and looked out over a valley bathed in silver moonlight. The stars shimmered overhead, and in that serene moment, he felt the weight of despair lift, replaced by a cautious hope that even in a broken world, life could persist.

Kota nudged him, drawing his attention back to the present. The dog's gaze was fixed on a narrow trail winding through a stand of ancient, gnarled trees that clung stubbornly to life amidst the rocky soil.

"Maybe there's shelter there," Ryo murmured, a note of optimism threading through his voice. He adjusted his pack and led the way down the winding trail, the path illuminated by the soft glow of bioluminescent fungi that adorned the tree trunks—a reminder that nature, even in its most desolate forms, could adapt and survive.

The trail twisted through the trees like a secret passage, and soon Ryo found himself in a small clearing. In the centre stood a dilapidated structure, its walls overgrown with ivy and its roof partially caved in. It looked like an old watchtower or a guard post—a relic from a time when men built monuments to protect against the unknown. Now, it offered nothing more than shelter from the biting cold and a temporary haven from the uncertainties of the Wastes. Inside the structure, Ryo and Kota settled down.

Ryo built a small fire using remnants of driftwood and dried brush, the flames casting flickering shadows on the walls. He sat on a rough-hewn bench, pulling out the shard he'd collected earlier to examine it in the firelight. Its blue glow pulsed softly, as if in rhythm with the beating of his heart, and for a moment, Ryo was lost in thought. The shard, the encounters with the Rift Hunters, and even the strange whispers of the Wastes all melded into a tapestry of mystery—a tapestry that hinted at a larger destiny he had yet to understand. Kota lay near his feet, eyes half-closed but ever-watchful.

The quiet of the night was punctuated only by the crackle of the fire and the occasional rustle of the wind. In that moment of relative calm, Ryo allowed himself to reflect on the journey so far.

Every step through the Wastes was a battle against both external threats and the internal spectre of hopelessness. Yet here, in this fragile refuge, he found a small spark of hope—a belief that somewhere beyond the desolation lay the answers to the mystery of time's fracture, and perhaps a path to redemption.

As the fire dwindled to glowing embers, Ryo wrapped himself in a threadbare blanket and settled in for a fitful sleep. His dreams were a collage of images—the chaotic clash of the Rift Hunters, the haunting visage of Kaori, and the gentle, reassuring eyes of Kota.

He dreamed of a time when the world was whole, when the light of the sun was unfiltered and time marched steadily onward. And in those dreams, the shard pulsed like a beacon, guiding him toward a future that was as uncertain as it was desperately needed.

Morning broke slowly over the horizon, the first rays of light piercing the darkness like fragile promises. Ryo awoke with a start, the chill of the new day seeping into his bones. Kota stirred beside him, yawning and stretching as if greeting the dawn with quiet enthusiasm. Ryo gathered his few belongings and, after stoking the small fire into a modest blaze, prepared to leave the shelter. The journey through the Wastes was far from over.

Today, the path ahead was unclear—a labyrinth of shifting sands, hidden dangers, and the constant threat of time distortions that could change everything in an instant. But as Ryo stepped out of the ancient watchtower, the sound of his footsteps mingled with the soft murmur of the wind, and he felt a determined resolve settling in his heart.

"There's more to this world than despair, isn't there, Kota?" he whispered, glancing down at his faithful companion. The dog's bright eyes met his with an intensity that spoke of loyalty and courage. Together, they stepped forward, leaving behind the temporary shelter and venturing back into the vast, unpredictable Wastes.

Though the dangers of the Wastes were many and the future uncertain, Ryo knew that as long as he had Kota by his side, he would never walk alone. And so, with the rising sun lighting a path through the chaos, Ryo and Kota disappeared into the endless area of the Wastes—two souls bound by fate, driven by an unyielding determination to survive, and united in their quest to reclaim a future from the ruins of the past.

Chapter 6: Phantom Haven

The wasteland's oppressive silence was broken only by the whisper of wind over cracked earth and the distant, intermittent hum of time anomalies. After days of trudging through the desolate region following their harrowing escape from the urban ruins, Ryo and Kota pressed on, their weary feet leading them ever deeper into the unknown. The landscape shifted gradually from endless broken pavement to wide stretches of barren land flecked with scrub and the occasional rock outcropping.

Yet even as they walked, Ryo's eyes caught something unusual in the distance—a flicker of movement that seemed almost like an illusion. At first, it appeared as a ripple on the horizon—a wavering shimmer that danced under the heavy afternoon sun. Ryo slowed his pace, squinting against the glare.

"Kota, do you see that?" he asked softly. The Shiba Inu's ears perked up, and he tilted his head in the direction Ryo indicated, his nose twitching as if trying to catch a scent carried in the wind.

As they approached, the rippling shimmer coalesced into the faint outline of a village. It was as if the very air had conspired to form a silhouette—a cluster of crumbling buildings, a central square, and a few scattered figures going about their day. But as soon as Ryo and Kota drew near, the vision began to distort.

The outlines wavered, and for an instant, the village seemed to vanish into the heat of the midday sun, only to reappear when the pair reached its edge. Ryo's heart quickened. He had heard whispers of "Mirage Villages" from other survivors—places trapped in the folds of time, where the same day played out over and over, impervious to the chaos of the outside world.

With cautious steps, he led Kota toward the village, determined to uncover its secrets. The closer they got, the more details emerged: a row of modest houses with faded facades, a cobblestone square where an old fountain sat dry and cracked, and inhabitants who moved with a quiet, almost mechanical rhythm, as if following a script they did not understand. When Ryo and Kota crossed the threshold into the village, the atmosphere shifted dramatically. The heat and dust of the Wastes were replaced by a cool, almost surreal calm.

The sound of distant traffic and the drone of city life were nowhere to be heard—instead, the gentle murmur of conversation and the occasional clink of a glass cup provided a background score to the day. Yet there was an eerie quality to it all, a sense that time had become fixed, locked in an endless loop. A middle-aged woman in a faded dress swept the front steps of a modest cottage as if on cue. Her movements were precise, repetitive; with each sweep of her broom, she seemed to retrace the same action over and over. Ryo stopped, watching her in silence, while Kota sniffed at the ground curiously. He trotted closer to the woman, his head bowed in polite curiosity. The woman looked up and smiled—a smile that was both warm and haunted, as though it carried the weight of decades. But before she could speak, a voice called out from across the square.

"Morning, dear," said an elderly man, leaning on a weathered cane as he walked past a row of houses. His voice was gentle but carried an undeniable note of resignation. The inhabitants, though few, went about their day in a rhythm that felt both timeless and tragic. Every face, every gesture, was suspended in a moment that repeated itself without change.

Ryo felt an inexplicable pull toward the centre of the village. Though he was a wary traveler hardened by the collapse of his world, the surreal calm and the repetitive nature of the scene stirred something deep within him—both hope and sorrow. He stepped forward, carefully observing the villagers. They moved in silent synchrony, as if they were actors on a stage, performing a play that had been rehearsed countless times. Their eyes were distant, as though they were not fully aware of their surroundings. Kota, meanwhile, wandered toward a small cluster of houses at the edge of the square. He paused in front of a weathered door and let out a soft whine. Ryo hurried over, feeling the urgency in his companion's eyes.

"What is it, boy?" he murmured. As he reached out to open the door, it swung open with a creak as if welcoming him. Inside, the space was dimly lit by the soft glow of a single lamp. A frail old man sat in a rocking chair, his eyes fixed on a faded photograph clutched in his wrinkled hands. Ryo stepped inside cautiously.

"Sir, I mean no harm. I'm just passing through." The old man didn't immediately respond; his eyes, heavy with unspoken memories, slowly met Ryo's.

"You're new, not from around here, I reckon." He finally said in a raspy voice. Ryo nodded.

"No, I'm not. I'm Ryo, and this is Kota. We've been traveling for some time." The old man gave a small, sad smile.

"I'm Elias. I've been here as long as I can remember. This village... it's a mirage, it's our mirage, our prison and our sanctuary all at once." He paused, his gaze drifting to the photograph in his hands.

"Every day, the same things happen. We live, work, wait—unaware that time has stopped turning." Ryo, intrigued by Elias's words.

71

"Stopped turning?" he repeated softly. Elias nodded slowly.

"Yes. Ever since the Time Rapture, many places have been touched by time in strange ways. Some are shattered beyond repair; others, like this village, have been caught in a loop—a single day repeated again and again. I don't know how it happened, only that we are bound by it. We're trapped in a moment that never ends." Outside, the sounds of the village's repetitive routine echoed faintly—a woman sweeping the same porch, a child running in circles, an elderly couple walking hand in hand along the same path. Ryo felt a chill at the thought. The very idea of living the same day over and over, without change, without progress, was both horrifying and heartbreakingly tragic.

As Ryo left Elias's modest home, his mind churned with questions. Was this village a natural consequence of the Time Rapture—a pocket of the past frozen in time? Or was it an anomaly, a place where time had been deliberately, or perhaps mysteriously, halted? His gaze fell to the shard he had hidden away, its soft blue glow pulsing in his pocket. Could it be that these fragments of time were connected, that this mirage village was yet another echo of the shattered timeline? Kota padded at his side as Ryo made his way back into the square.

The villagers continued their eternal routines, oblivious to his presence, their expressions blank and resigned. In the distance, the sky shimmered with hints of distant rifts—a reminder that outside the borders of this timeless trap, the world still roiled in chaos. Ryo climbed a small set of steps leading to what appeared to be the village's central hall—a modest building adorned with peeling murals depicting happier times.

He pushed open the heavy door and entered a room filled with subdued light and an overwhelming sense of melancholy. The air was cool and still, and in one corner, a delicate clock hung on the wall, its hands frozen at exactly 10:10. Ryo could almost feel the weight of every lost second in that stillness. An elderly woman sat at a table near the clock, methodically arranging a set of old, faded letters and photographs. When Ryo entered, she looked up, her eyes deep and knowing.

"Welcome, traveler," she said softly.

"I am Miriam." Ryo offered a cautious smile.

"Hello, Miriam. I'm Ryo, and this is Kota." The woman's eyes lingered on the dog for a moment before returning to Ryo.

"You do not look like you belong to a day that never changes," she observed gently.

"You carry the weariness of a world in motion—a world that remembers change, even if we do not." Ryo felt the weight of her words settle in his chest.

"I've been on the move for a long time," he admitted.

"But now that I'm here… it feels like I've stepped into something I wasn't meant to. Like the air itself won't let go." Miriam's expression softened.

"That's how it begins. You're not trapped the way we are—not yet. But the village… it tries to pull others into its rhythm. A loop that preserves memory but denies change. We are echoes of ourselves, reliving a day that's long gone." Ryo's eyes drifted to the clock, its hands unmoving.

"And you? Have you ever tried to break free?" Miriam sighed, her gaze returning to the scattered letters.

"Many times," she said.

"I record each moment, hoping something will break the pattern. But every sunrise resets us. Only fragments remain. The past wants to be remembered—but it refuses to move forward."

Ryo's thoughts turned to Kota. The Shiba Inu had always seemed to sense distortions others couldn't.

"Have you noticed anything… strange about the dog?" he asked. Miriam's eyes widened.

"Yes. There's a vibrancy to him. A frequency that doesn't match this place. I've seen him near the old clock tower, where time grows thin and the rift flickers like a dying star. Some believe he's not bound by time the way we are. That he carries a spark—something ancient, something alive." Ryo's pulse quickened. Kaori's cryptic warnings echoed in his mind.

"If he's connected to all this… what must I do?" Miriam looked at him with compassion and sorrow.

"Understand the loop. Seek out the remnants—old records, forgotten signs. There's a shard hidden in the central square that may hold a clue. And trust your companion. In him, time still moves. And through him, so might you."

Ryo nodded slowly, absorbing her words. As the day wore on, he wandered through the village, taking note of every detail—the patterned movements of the villagers, the static smiles, and the uncanny precision of their daily routines.

It was as if each moment was meticulously repeated, a loop that had imprisoned their very souls. Meanwhile, Kota seemed increasingly drawn to the edges of the square. At one point, the dog slipped away from Ryo and approached a weathered stone bench where a small, intricately carved object lay half-buried in the dust. Ryo hurried after him, finding Kota pawing at the object with gentle insistence. It was a time shard, the one Miriam mentioned, distinct from the ones he had encountered before: its surface was etched with delicate symbols and it pulsed with a soft, amber glow.

Ryo picked it up carefully, feeling a surge of energy ripple through his fingertips. The shard seemed to vibrate in harmony with Kota's quiet whines, as if it recognized something in the dog—a connection that defied explanation. In that moment, a series of fragmented visions burst through Ryo's mind. He saw flashes of the past: a bustling market street where children laughed and played, the vibrant hues of a sunset unspoiled by ruin, and a fleeting image of Kota as a young puppy, full of life and untamed spirit. The visions were disjointed and overwhelming, leaving Ryo gasping as he clutched the shard to his chest.

Overwhelmed by the sudden influx of memories and possibilities, Ryo staggered to a nearby bench and sat down, Kota curling up by his side. He took a deep breath and tried to steady his racing heart. The shard's glow pulsed steadily, and with each beat, Ryo felt as if time itself were whispering secrets to him—a promise that within the endless repetition of this day lay the keys to a different future. In the quiet hours that followed, Ryo spent what felt like an eternity with the shard and his thoughts.

He began to jot down notes in a battered notebook he kept in his bag pack—snippets of conversation overheard from villagers, vague recollections of times past, and the strange patterns he had observed in the loop. Each word was a desperate attempt to piece together the puzzle of the Mirage Village, to understand why time here stood still and how it might one day be set free.

As dusk approached, the village's inhabitants continued their unchanging routines. The gentle clinking of cups at a corner café, the soft murmur of a conversation at a window seat, and the quiet determination of a street sweeper all repeated with mechanical precision.

Yet, amidst this routine, Ryo could sense an undercurrent of longing—a desire, perhaps, to break free of the cycle, to experience even one moment of true change. The sky turned from a pale blue to a deep indigo, and lamplight flickered in the windows of the small houses. Ryo gathered his notes and the shard, tucking them safely away.

"There's a pattern here," he whispered to Kota, who looked up at him with eyes that seemed to hold more wisdom than any man's.

"And I'm going to find it." Before leaving the square, Ryo took one last look at the central clock—a grand, ornate timepiece that hung on the wall of what appeared to be an old town hall. Its hands were frozen at 10:10, a silent sentinel to the passage of countless identical days. As he stared at it, the shard in his pocket pulsated, as if urging him to unlock the secret it guarded. Stepping out into the cool night, Ryo felt the weight of destiny pressing upon him.

The Mirage Village, with its eternal loop, was both a prison and a treasure trove of forgotten histories. If he could decipher its patterns, if he could harness the memories it preserved, perhaps there was a way not only to break free of the endless day in the Mirage Village but also to restore something of the lost time. Kota padded at his side as they walked away from the village, the rhythmic murmurs of its inhabitants fading into the distance behind them.

Ryo's mind churned with possibilities and unanswered questions. How had this village become ensnared in a time loop? What was the origin of the shard, and how did it connect to the larger tapestry of the Time Rapture? And, most importantly, how did Kota—a creature of unfathomable loyalty and mysterious power—fit into all of this? The journey ahead was shrouded in uncertainty. The Mirage Village was only a small piece of the vast, fractured puzzle that was Ryo's world. Yet, in its stillness and its repetition lay clues—clues that might one day lead to the restoration of time or, at the very least, a better understanding of the chaos that had consumed it.

As the night deepened, Ryo and Kota moved onward, leaving behind the hypnotic, eternal rhythm of the Mirage Village. The shard's soft glow continued to pulse within his jacket, a quiet reminder of the mysteries waiting to be unraveled. In the silent dark, amid the shifting sands of the Wastes and the echo of a day that repeated itself without end, Ryo vowed to uncover the secrets of time—no matter the cost.

With each step, he carried the hope that, one day, the clock would start again. That the mirage of a better future might become a reality, and that the bond he shared with Kota would be the spark to ignite a change in a world where time had long been lost.

And so, beneath a sky scattered with ancient stars, Ryo and Kota ventured forth into the unknown, their path illuminated by the faint, steady pulse of a shard that held within it the echoes of countless yesterdays and the promise of tomorrow yet to come.

Chapter 7: Heart of Time

The day broke with a restless sky as Ryo and Kota trudged from the Mirage Village. Though the village's endless loop had faded behind them, its haunting echoes remained, lingering in Ryo's thoughts like an unanswered question. In the aftermath of that surreal place, where time had stood frozen and memories were re-lived with every passing moment, Ryo's mind was heavy with the weight of possibility—and foreboding. The barren road before them stretched into a horizon broken by jagged mountains and streaks of fractured light where distant rifts danced like fleeting ghosts.

Kota padded steadily at Ryo's side, his eyes alert and his movements purposeful. For the first time since their arduous journey began, Ryo felt that something fundamental was stirring beneath the surface of his world—something that might explain the inexplicable bond between man and dog that had carried him through the desolation.

It was during a long, silent trek through a valley of wind-sculpted rocks and crumbling ruins that Ryo first noticed a subtle change. The air seemed charged with a quiet energy, the very atmosphere vibrating with a rhythm that felt almost… alive. As they climbed a steep ridge, the uneven ground gave way to a plateau where the remnants of an old clock tower jutted from the earth. Its Stone face was scarred by time and neglect, yet inexplicably, the broken clock hands pointed to a precise moment—10:10—a detail that had haunted him since his first glimpse of a halted clock in the Mirage Village.

Ryo stopped at the edge of the plateau and knelt on the cool stone, his eyes tracing the ancient carvings that decorated the tower's exterior. He reached into his jacket pocket and retrieved the blue shard he had collected in the ruins earlier—a fragment that pulsed softly in the morning light. As he held it aloft, the shard's gentle glow seemed to harmonize with the steady throb of the earth beneath him. It was then that he began to notice something extraordinary: where Kota stood, the air shimmered faintly, and the distortions that so often marred the landscape appeared to settle into a brief, fragile calm.

"Kota…" Ryo murmured, gazing at his faithful companion. The dog lifted his head and met his eyes that made Ryo's heart skip a beat. For a moment, time itself seemed to pause, as if listening to an unspoken message. He slowly extended a hand, almost reverently, toward Kota. In that gesture, something unspoken passed between them—a silent understanding that went beyond loyalty or companionship. It was as if Kota's very presence was a counterbalance to the chaotic rifts that fractured their world.

The phenomenon deepened as Ryo observed a small rift that had formed near the base of the tower. Usually, such anomalies churned with violent, unpredictable energy; however, as Kota approached its edge, the rift's turbulent currents slowed, and its chaotic colours softened into a harmonious blend of blues and greens. Ryo's eyes widened as he realized that the dog was, in effect, stabilizing the fracture—a living fulcrum upon which time balanced. Ryo's thoughts whirled. Could it be that all the subtle signs—the strange warmth that sometimes emanated from Kota, the occasional shimmering of the air around him—were not random occurrences?

Had he always been in the presence of something far greater than a mere pet? The answer, though dawning upon him, was as daunting as it was wondrous: Kota was the Timekeeper's Heart, a being whose existence resonated with the pulse of time itself. The realization filled Ryo with both awe and trepidation. He remembered the visions from the shard—the flickers of a past life, the echo of lost hope, and the surreal images of Kota as a puppy, carefree and vibrant. All those moments, now stitched together in his mind, formed a tapestry of destiny he had never anticipated. In the midst of chaos and despair, his loyal companion had become the linchpin of a cosmic order—a beacon capable of holding back the collapse of time.

Ryo sat back on the stone, his gaze fixed on the quiet miracle unfolding before him. The rift, once a seething vortex of chaotic energy, now shimmered gently, held in check by the silent power of Kota's presence. The air around them vibrated with a low, rhythmic hum, as if echoing the steady beat of a colossal, unseen clock. For a long moment, the valley was silent—an interlude in the discord of shattered time. Then Ryo spoke softly,

"Kota... you're more than I ever imagined. You're... you're the heart of time itself." His voice trembled with a mix of wonder and sorrow. It was as if acknowledging this truth would change everything—both for him and for the fragile world they inhabited. Kota cocked his head, as if in response, and then trotted over to where the shard lay partially buried in the dust.

Ryo followed, feeling that the shard, too, was reacting to this moment of revelation. He knelt and retrieved it, holding it next to Kota's paw. The shard pulsed more vividly now, its soft blue light mingling with the subtle glow that seemed to emanate from Kota's fur. Ryo's eyes stung with unshed tears as he whispered,

"You've always been our saving grace, haven't you, boy?" In that moment, Ryo felt an overwhelming surge of determination.

If Kota was indeed the Timekeeper's Heart—a living anchor for a world on the brink of temporal collapse—then he could not allow anyone to exploit that power. The words of the Rift Hunters, the dark ambitions of those who sought to harness the chaos, now took on a new, ominous meaning. Ryo vowed to protect Kota at all costs, not only for his own sake but for the sake of a future that might yet be restored. Ryo rose slowly and began to make his way back down the ridge, his mind racing with questions and possibilities.

The vision of the stabilized rift, the quiet miracle of Kota's influence on time, would be a secret he carried close to his heart—a beacon of hope amid the desolation. Yet with this hope came a terrible responsibility. The knowledge that Kota was the Timekeeper's Heart also meant that his very existence was a target for those who wished to control time, to bend it to their own dark ends.

As Ryo descended, the landscape around him seemed to shift subtly. Where once there had been harsh, chaotic distortions, the air near Kota now held a fleeting calm, as though the dog's presence softened the relentless assault of fractured time. Shadows played gently over the ground, and even the distant rifts seemed less violent—an intermission in the constant battle for the soul of time. They reached a narrow, winding path that led toward the outskirts of a ruined city.

The sun was climbing higher now, its light scattering the last remnants of night. Ryo's thoughts were a turbulent mix of wonder, fear, and resolve. Each step was accompanied by the silent beat of Kota's steady pace—a heartbeat that, he now believed, echoed through the corridors of time itself. Along the way, they encountered other survivors—haggard figures whose eyes held stories of loss and desperation.

One elderly man, leaning on a splintered cane, stopped and stared at Kota with a mix of reverence and disbelief.

"That dog... he's different," the man muttered before shuffling away. Others gave similar glances—covert, awed looks that hinted at rumours and legends whispered in hushed tones amid the ruins. By midday, Ryo found himself standing before the entrance of an old, crumbling archive—a library that had once been a repository of knowledge. Its vast halls, now silent and overgrown with vines, promised secrets of the past. Ryo hesitated at the threshold, the weight of his newfound understanding heavy on his shoulders. Inside, he believed, lay clues to the origin of the Time Rapture, and perhaps even the means to harness the power of the Timekeeper's Heart.

"Kota, come on," Ryo said, determination lacing his voice.

"We have answers to find." The dog padded eagerly beside him, as if aware that their journey was about to take a decisive turn.

Inside the library, dust motes danced in the streams of sunlight that pierced through broken windows. Rows upon rows of books—yellowed with age and forgotten by time—lined the walls.

Ryo moved carefully among the towering shelves, his fingers brushing against the spines of ancient books, each one a silent witness to a lost era. The atmosphere was thick with the scent of aged paper and the faint echo of voices long silenced. He found a section dedicated to history and science—a collection of works that once attempted to explain the nature of time and the cosmos. One volume, bound in worn leather and embossed with intricate symbols, caught his eye.

He pulled it from the shelf and carefully opened it, revealing faded diagrams and cryptic annotations about temporal energy, rifts, and the possibility of "living anchors" that could stabilize time. Ryo's breath caught as he read passages that eerily mirrored his own experiences with Kota. The text spoke of a "heart" that could resonate with the very fabric of time—a force that, if nurtured, might restore balance to a fractured existence.

Outside, the wind began to pick up, rustling through the broken leaves and scattering fragments of paper across the ancient floor. Ryo clutched the book tightly, feeling as though he had uncovered a crucial piece of a puzzle that spanned beyond the confines of his shattered world. The library, though falling apart around him, pulsed with a latent promise—a promise that knowledge, even in the midst of ruin, could be a powerful tool.

Ryo spent hours poring over the fragile pages, cross-referencing notes and piecing together fragments of forgotten knowledge. Every now and then, he would glance over at Kota, who sat calmly at his feet, as if guarding the man's thoughts. In those moments, Ryo felt a profound connection—a reassurance that his loyal companion was not just a bystander but a key player in the unfolding saga of time.

The day waned as Ryo emerged from the library, the old leather book clutched in his arm and new determination burning in his eyes.

The path ahead was uncertain, but he now carried a spark of understanding—a glimpse of how Kota's unique essence might be harnessed to restore order. The Timekeeper's Heart was not merely a title; it was a truth, woven into the very DNA of his companion. As dusk approached, the sky transformed into a tapestry of deep purples and fiery oranges. Ryo and Kota set out once again, leaving behind the sanctuary of the library for the uncertain wilds beyond. Every step they took resonated with a quiet urgency; the lessons of the day had etched themselves into Ryo's soul, compelling him forward into the night.

In the twilight, the landscape seemed to shimmer with an otherworldly glow, as if the very fabric of reality was on the brink of revealing its hidden truths. Ryo's mind churned with possibilities and lingering questions: How could he harness this power? Could the legends be true? And what price would be required to safeguard the delicate balance of time?

Kota led the way with unwavering purpose, occasionally pausing as if to listen to whispers only he could hear. Ryo followed, the ancient book clutched tightly to his chest—a silent promise that he would uncover the secrets behind the Time Rapture and his companion's extraordinary gift. As they traversed the fractured landscape, the rifts overhead pulsed intermittently—a gentle reminder that time was still in flux. Yet in the calm that emanated from Kota, there was a stability that defied the chaos. Ryo began to believe that the bond between them was more than mere companionship; it was a living, breathing force capable of mending the fractures of existence.

The knowledge gleaned from the library, the whispered legends, and the undeniable signs in the landscape would guide him on a path that could, one day, restore balance to a world that had long been fractured by the collapse of time.

As the first stars began to twinkle in the deepening sky, Ryo paused at a crossroads—a narrow path leading into a dense thicket of ancient trees, and a broader, open road stretching into the uncertain distance. He knelt beside Kota, gently stroking the dog's fur, and spoke softly,

"We're in this together, boy. Whatever comes next, we'll face it side by side." Kota's eyes shone with a steady light as if affirming his silent promise. Ryo rose and stepped onto the chosen path, the ancient book tucked securely in his pack, the lessons of the day etched in his heart, and Kota's gentle presence guiding him like a living compass.

Together, they moved forward into the deepening night, embarking on a journey that would test the limits of their courage and unravel the mysteries of time—one fragile, determined step at a time.

Chapter 8: Silent Horizon

The wind over the wasteland had grown colder, carrying with it a sense of foreboding as dusk approached. Ryo and Kota had been following a narrow, winding road for hours—a path that meandered through a zone where the fabric of time seemed thin and unstable. Every so often, the air shimmered with unnatural light, as if the boundaries between moments were dissolving. Ryo's thoughts churned with the knowledge that in these regions, danger was not only human but also a matter of time itself.

As the pair crested a small rise, the landscape opened into a vast, barren plain scarred with deep fissures in the earth. In the centre of the plain, a swirling vortex of light and shadow pulsed in the distance—a rift, larger and more volatile than any they had seen before. The rift's edges flickered with a palette of shifting colours, and its presence warped the air, distorting both sound and vision.

"Look, Kota," Ryo whispered, his voice barely audible over the restless wind. The dog's ears twitched and his eyes narrowed as he fixed his gaze on the vortex. Ryo had long learned to trust the silent warnings of his loyal companion, and now a chill ran down his spine as he realized that the rift was drawing them in. Before he could decide whether to retreat or press on, a sudden, discordant sound shattered the uneasy calm.

From behind a clump of jagged rocks at the edge of the plain, several figures emerged, moving with deliberate, predatory precision. Their armour was mismatched yet functional—patchworks of scavenged metal and leather—and each carried a weapon that glinted menacingly in the low light.

These were the Rift Hunters, a ruthless band that had been tracking anomalies and exploiting the fractured timelines for their own gain. Ryo's heart pounded as he pressed himself lower to the ground, pulling Kota close.

The Rift Hunters' leader—a tall, gaunt figure with eyes that burned like embers—stepped forward, his voice cutting through the wind with icy authority.

"You have wandered into dangerous territory," the leader said, his tone both mocking and commanding.

"The rifts do not forgive, and neither do we." Ryo's hand had tightened around his makeshift spear.

"We're just passing through," he replied, his voice steady despite the adrenaline surging in his veins.

"We're not looking for trouble." A cold laugh emanated from the leader.

"Trouble finds you when you stray from the safe paths," he said.

"And it seems you've strayed right into our hunting ground."

Before Ryo could react further, another Rift Hunter darted forward from the shadows. The assailant's movements were swift—a blur of motion—and before Ryo could lift his weapon, the figure lunged toward Kota. A cry of alarm tore from Ryo's throat as he sprang up, spear thrusting forward, meeting the attacker mid-swing. In the ensuing chaos, the world around them seemed to fracture further.

The rift in the distance pulsed violently, its light growing erratic. For a split second, the unstable energies of the rift began to seep toward the combatants, distorting the air and warping the sounds of battle. Voices overlapped in dissonant echoes—a past cry, a future whisper, and a present roar all merging into one racket. Ryo gritted his teeth as he parried a vicious strike aimed at his midsection.

He could feel the raw energy of the rift tugging at the edges of his perception. The ground beneath his feet trembled, and for a moment, time itself seemed to hesitate. In that fractured instant, he caught a glimpse of something unimaginable: silhouettes of figures from his own past, ghosts of memories long buried, drifting in and out of focus like mirages.

"Kota, stay with me!" he shouted, glancing

down at the dog as he fended off another blow. Kota, eyes wide with both fear and fierce determination, countered with a snarl and a leap that sent him crashing into one of the approaching Rift Hunters. The attacker staggered back, clutching his wounded arm, and Ryo seized the opportunity to push forward.

The Rift Hunters, taken aback by the unexpected ferocity of Kota's defence, hesitated for a heartbeat—a heartbeat that stretched into an eternity as the rift's chaotic energies intensified. The leader's eyes flashed with anger as he barked orders, and more figures emerged from the surrounding darkness to join the fray.

The battle erupted anew, each clash of weapons punctuating the disorienting pulse of the rift. Amid the commotion, Ryo became acutely aware of something extraordinary. As he fought desperately to protect himself and Kota, he noticed that the area immediately around the dog was changing. The wild, erratic energies of the rift seemed to recoil whenever Kota moved close, as if the very fabric of time acknowledged his presence. The chaotic distortions in the air stilled momentarily, and even the overlapping voices of past and future grew quieter, replaced by a low, rhythmic hum. Ryo's mind raced. He had long suspected that Kota was more than a loyal companion—that his very being resonated with a power tied to the fractured nature of time. Now, in the midst of battle, it was unmistakable.

Kota's presence created a small pocket of calm amid the storm, a living sanctuary that even the violent energies of the rift could not completely disrupt. Emboldened by this realization, Ryo redoubled his efforts.

"I won't let you take him!" he shouted, his voice echoing off the crumbling walls of the plain. With a series of swift, calculated moves, he parried a blow aimed at his shoulder and counterattacked with a force born of desperation and newfound resolve. His spear found its mark, and one of the attackers crumpled to the ground with a pained cry. Yet the battle was far from over. The Hunters regrouped, their eyes glinting with merciless intent as they advanced. The leader's voice rang out again, laced with venom,

"You think your pet can protect you? He is nothing more than a tool to harness the chaos. Surrender him, and we may let you live." Ryo's blood surged with indignation.

"I will never surrender Kota," he declared, voice trembling with a mix of rage and determination.

"He is my family—and he's the heart of a hope that you can't understand!" At those words, the air around them seemed to ripple even more violently.

The rift, which was visible in the distant, flared with intense light. Its chaotic energy surged forward. For a long, breathless moment, the battlefield fell into an eerie stillness. The Hunters, caught between their lust for power and the unyielding bond between man and dog, faltered in their advance. In that moment of suspended time, Ryo felt an overwhelming clarity. The rift's energy, which had threatened to tear the world apart, now swirled in a controlled rhythm around Kota. The phenomenon was unmistakable: Kota was acting as a stabilizing force, a beacon of calm that held the turbulent forces at bay.

Ryo could almost feel the heartbeat of time itself synchronizing with the steady beat of his loyal companion's presence. Seizing the opportunity, Ryo surged forward with renewed vigour.

"Run!" he cried, not just for himself but for Kota as well. With a fierce determination, he drove his spear at an advancing foe, knocking him aside as he made a break for cover behind a cluster of jagged rocks. The Rift Hunters, disoriented by the sudden shift in the rift's behaviour and the defiant resistance of their target, hesitated. Their leader bellowed in frustration as more of his comrades fell back into the encroaching darkness. The chaotic dance of the rift's energies provided Ryo and Kota with a fleeting window of escape.

They bolted across the plain, their silhouettes merging with the shadows as the violent clamour of battle faded behind them. For what felt like an eternity, they ran. The world around them was a blur of fractured light and shifting darkness—a place where the boundaries between past and present dissolved with every desperate step. Ryo's lungs burned with exertion, and his heart hammered in his chest, but he could not slow down. Every instinct told him that the safety of the rift's pocket—where Kota's stabilizing power was most evident—was the only refuge from the relentless pursuit of their enemies. At last, they reached the edge of a rocky outcrop that jutted from the plain like a natural barricade.

Here, the ground was uneven and treacherous, but it offered concealment among its crags and crevices. Ryo quickly pressed himself against a rocky wall, dragging Kota down beside him. They huddled in silence, the echoes of battle still resonating faintly in the distance. The rift loomed in the sky—a turbulent, ever-shifting vortex of light and shadow—its energies still swirling unpredictably, yet somehow contained by the dog's presence. Ryo's chest heaved as he tried to catch his breath. His mind raced with questions and fears. These Rift Hunters were formidable, driven by an insatiable hunger for the power that lay hidden in the fractures of time. And now, more than ever, he understood that Kota was the target of their dark ambitions. Every moment that passed in this unstable region brought them closer to a confrontation that could decide not only their fate but the fate of time itself.

"Stay with me, Kota," Ryo murmured, gently stroking the dog's fur. In the dim light, he could see the quiet strength in Kota's eyes—the same unwavering loyalty that had carried them through so many trials. The bond between them was visible, a silent promise that transcended the chaos of the world. It was that very bond that had momentarily tamed the rift's wild energies, offering a glimpse of hope amid the encroaching darkness. As the distant sounds of battle receded into the night, Ryo allowed himself a moment to reflect on what had transpired.

The rift, with all its destructive potential, had become a mirror to his own inner turmoil—a reminder that in a world where time had been shattered, every heartbeat, every breath, was a struggle against the relentless pull of chaos. Yet, in the midst of that chaos, Kota's presence shone like a beacon—a living, breathing symbol of the possibility of order and renewal. The minutes stretched into what felt like hours as Ryo and Kota remained hidden in their rocky refuge.

The night deepened, and the first stars began to pierce the veil of darkness overhead. Slowly, the thunderous energy of the rift subsided to a low, rhythmic pulse—almost as if it were settling into a tentative calm. Ryo's mind, though still racing, began to find a measure of clarity in that quiet interval. He knew that their reprieve was temporary. The Hunters would regroup, and the rift would flare up again in a display of destructive power.

But for now, in the embrace of the rocky outcrop and under a sky studded with fragile stars, Ryo allowed himself to acknowledge the truth that had been revealed in the heat of battle: Kota was not just a dog, and he was not merely a companion. He was the Timekeeper's Heart—a living force that resonated with the pulse of time, capable of both mending and destroying the very fabric of reality. With a slow, deliberate breath, Ryo resolved to protect this precious spark at all costs.

"We're not done yet, boy," he whispered, determination hardening his voice.

"I won't let them take you. Not now, not ever."

In the darkness, Kota's eyes glowed softly, and for a moment, it was as if time itself acknowledged the solemn vow. The rift overhead pulsed on—a restless, unpredictable beacon—

and the distant echoes of enemy voices were swallowed by the night.

Ryo and Kota remained motionless in their rocky hideout, bound together by a fate that was only beginning to unfold. Eventually, the murmurs of distant pursuit began to fade, and the unstable energies in the sky receded into a muted hum. Ryo knew it was time to move. Carefully, he rose from his hiding place, mindful of every sound and shadow, and roused Kota. Together, they crept from behind the outcrop, the cool night air filling their lungs as they resumed their journey. Each step forward was measured and cautious.

The landscape around them, though scarred and desolate, held pockets of strange beauty—a field of wild, resilient flowers pushing through cracked earth, a slow-moving cloud of dust illuminated by the moon's gentle glow, and the steady, almost musical pulse of the rift in the distance. These moments of quiet wonder were fleeting.

As Ryo and Kota navigated a narrow canyon formed by towering rock walls, Ryo's mind remained fixated on the events of the evening. The battle with the Rift Hunters, the chaotic surge of the rift, and the undeniable power emanating from Kota—all of it wove together into a tapestry of destiny that he was only beginning to comprehend.

The canyon eventually opened up onto a broad, moonlit plain. The rift in the sky loomed like a distant, restless storm—its surface a chaotic dance of light and shadow. Ryo paused at the edge of the plain, glancing back at the dark canyon behind them.

"We keep moving," he murmured to Kota.

"We have to get further away from here before they find us again." Kota barked softly, as if in agreement, and together they set off across the open plain. The night was quiet except for the soft crunch of their footsteps and the distant, low hum of the rift's energy. Ryo's thoughts were a mixture of determination and trepidation.

The memory of the Hunters' threats, the surreal calm that had enveloped them when Kota's presence had tamed the rift, and the weight of the knowledge that his loyal companion was the Timekeeper's Heart—it was almost too much to bear. But as the first hints of dawn began to colour the edges of the sky with soft blues and purples, Ryo steeled himself for the challenges that lay ahead.

Every moment in the fractured landscape was a battle against chaos, and every heartbeat was a testament to their will to survive. The rift overhead pulsed with a subdued intensity, and the landscape, though scarred and uncertain, glimmered with the promise of a new beginning.

"Hold on, Kota," Ryo whispered, his voice resolute.

"We're not done yet. We have a future to reclaim." And so, under the watchful glow of a tentative dawn, Ryo and his faithful companion pressed onward.

Chapter 9: Fragments of Tomorrow

Ryo trudged along a cracked boulevard as twilight began to shroud the ruins of the old city. Every step seemed to echo with the weight of the past, and yet, amidst the decay, there were glimmers of what might have been—or might yet be. Kota, ever vigilant, padded at his side, his ears twitching as if listening for whispers from another time. Earlier that day, while traversing a deserted sector on the edge of the fractured metropolis, Ryo had discovered something remarkable. In a forgotten courtyard, hidden behind the remnants of a collapsed building, lay a time shard unlike any he had seen before. Its surface glowed with a soft, pale light—translucent and shifting, as if capturing fragments of memories in its depths.

Despite the danger inherent in such relics, Ryo had carefully pocketed the shard, unaware that it would soon unravel visions of a future that would shake the very core of his being. Now, as dusk turned the sky to deep indigo and the stars began to pierce the veil of darkness, Ryo found a quiet spot among the rubble—a crumbling bench in a vacant plaza—and settled down with Kota curling near his feet. With trembling hands, he retrieved the shard from his jacket and held it close to his face. At first, it was just a soft glow, but then the light deepened, pulsating in time with his heartbeat.

In an instant, the world around him faded into darkness, and he was plunged into a vision. He saw a city bathed in brilliant light—a future where the ruins had been replaced by towering spires of glass and steel, where the scars of the Time Rapture had been healed.

The streets were alive with people whose faces were unburdened by sorrow, and laughter filled the air like music. Ryo saw himself walking these pristine avenues, his eyes alight with purpose and hope. But then, as quickly as it came, the vision shifted.

The light dimmed, and the vibrant scenes turned ghostly and uncertain. Now, he was a stranger wandering through a familiar yet distant place, a version of the city that lay somewhere between what had been and what might be. The buildings here bore the marks of time and neglect, yet they also shimmered with hints of renewal. He saw fragments of conversations: joyful greetings, sorrowful farewells, and murmurs of promise that he could not fully grasp.

Ryo blinked hard, and the vision began to splinter into multiple images. One showed him as a younger man, laughing with friends in a sunlit park—a memory that might have been real in another life. Another depicted him, older and wearier, standing on a bridge overlooking a river that sparkled with strange, luminescent hues.

In yet another fleeting moment, he saw Kota—not the steadfast dog he knew, but a younger, wilder version, frolicking in a meadow of impossibly green grass under a sky untainted by ruin. A deep, almost overwhelming melancholy and hope mingled in Ryo's chest.

He realized that the shard was not merely a window into the future or a repository of forgotten memories; it was a tapestry of possibilities—each image a potential path, each flicker a choice yet to be made. The visions did not tell him exactly what would be, but they whispered of the hope that lay in reclaiming a future from the wreckage of the past.

"Kota…" Ryo murmured softly, his voice trembling with a mix of wonder and sorrow. The loyal Shiba Inu stirred at his side, his eyes reflecting an unspoken understanding. In that moment, Ryo was acutely aware that every hope he had for a better tomorrow was intertwined with the bond he shared with his faithful companion. The vision began to fade, and the world slowly reasserted itself around Ryo.

The soft glow of the shard dimmed, leaving him in the cool twilight of the ruined plaza. For several long seconds, he sat in silence, absorbing the lingering echoes of the images that had danced before his eyes. Outside, the night deepened, and a gentle breeze stirred the dust, as if the world itself was exhaling after a long-held breath. Ryo carefully slipped the shard back into his pocket and looked down at Kota.

"What did you see, boy?" he whispered, though he knew the answer lay only in the unspoken bond between them.

Kota approached and rested his head on Ryo's knee, his eyes reflecting a calm assurance that belied the chaos of their world. In the aftermath of the vision, Ryo's mind churned with questions. What did these glimpses mean? Were they mere possibilities, or did they hold a deeper truth about the fractured timeline? He recalled Kaori's cryptic warning and the notion that time, once shattered, might be pieced together by those who were willing to search for the fragments of tomorrow. Now, with the shard's visions fresh in his mind, Ryo felt the stirrings of destiny calling him to action. He rose slowly, determination etched into every line of his weathered face.

"We have a future to chase, Kota," he said firmly, as if speaking to the very essence of hope.

"No matter how broken the past, there's a tomorrow waiting for us—if we can only find it."

The next few hours passed in a blur of restless motion and quiet reflection. Ryo and Kota resumed through the twilight-draped streets, the memory of the vision urging them onward.

Every step became a meditation on possibility—each ruined building, each flickering streetlight, a silent witness to the promise of change. In every shadow, Ryo sought the familiar contours of the future he had glimpsed, trying to piece together the fragments of a world that might yet be restored. As they passed through a narrow alley where the wind carried whispers of voices long silenced, Ryo found himself pausing to consider the nature of memory.

He remembered a time when memories were clear and unburdened by the weight of loss—a time when the past was a source of comfort rather than regret. The shard had shown him that memories, like pieces of time, could be both fragile and transformative. They held the power to illuminate a path forward, even in the darkest of nights. In a moment of quiet introspection, Ryo knelt by a weathered mural on a crumbling wall. The faded colours depicted scenes of a vibrant Community—families laughing, children playing, and elders sharing stories beneath a radiant sun. He traced a trembling finger along the mural's surface, feeling the cool relief of chipped paint beneath his touch.

"Maybe," he thought aloud,

"if we can reclaim even a single memory of what was, we might forge a future where tomorrow isn't just a dream."

Kota, sensing Ryo's moment of vulnerability, sat close by and rested his head on his lap. In that simple act, Ryo found solace—a reminder that the bond between them was unbroken, even as the world around them lay in ruins. They continued their journey, leaving the alley behind and merging onto a broader street where remnants of a once-bustling market still lingered. The neon signs that once flashed with life were now dark and silent, yet in their quiet stillness, they whispered of possibilities. Ryo's mind wandered back to the shard's visions—the sparkling river, the youthful crowds, and the image of Kota running free in an endless field.

Each fragment was a promise of renewal, a beacon that lit the way forward. As midnight approached, the city's chaos softened into a haunting quiet. Ryo and Kota found temporary refuge in an abandoned café whose windows were broken, but whose walls still bore murals of happier times. Inside, the remnants of tables and chairs were scattered about, and the scent of stale coffee mixed with the ever-present dust of decay. Ryo settled into a corner, pulling his coat tightly around him while Kota lay curled at his feet. There, in the half-light of the forsaken establishment, Ryo allowed himself to reflect on the visions from the shard. He scribbled notes in a battered journal he always carried—a desperate attempt to capture every fleeting detail, every half-remembered image that might hold the key to unlocking the future.

He wrote of the bustling city in sunlight, of quiet moments shared with loved ones, and of a world where time flowed smoothly once more. With each word, he felt a spark of hope kindle within him—a fragile, persistent light in a seemingly unending darkness. Outside, the distant hum of the fractured city mingled with the soft murmurs of the wind. Ryo glanced toward the door, half-expecting to see a figure from the visions—a stranger who might offer further insight or perhaps a warning. But the street remained empty, its silence both a comfort and a challenge. Kota stirred and nudged Ryo's hand, pulling him from his reverie.

"Come on, boy," Ryo said softly, rising to his feet.

"We need to keep moving." The night was deep, but the promise of a new tomorrow, however uncertain, urged them forward. Together, Ryo and Kota stepped back out into the deserted streets. As they made their way through the labyrinth of ruins, Ryo couldn't help but notice subtle signs of change in the fractured landscape. A building here showed fresh graffiti hinting at renewed hope; a small garden, hidden behind a broken fence, burst with stubborn green life. These small miracles—tiny assertions of resilience—fuelled his resolve.

Memories of tomorrow, however fleeting, were all around him, waiting to be embraced. The visions of the shard had offered him a glimpse of what might be possible—a world where the wounds of the past could be healed, where hope was not a relic of memory but a vibrant force capable of sparking change. With Kota by his side, Ryo set his course toward the distant light of a rising sun.

Each step was measured and deliberate, as if he were walking on the delicate strands of a new destiny. He would seek out the lost fragments of the past, piece together the scattered echoes of what once was, and use them to forge a path to a future where time was whole again.

"Tomorrow isn't just a dream," Ryo whispered to Kota, who gazed up at him with eyes full of quiet assurance.

"It's something we can build, step by step." And so, with the memories of yesterday guiding him and the promise of tomorrow lighting his way, Ryo and Kota embarked on the next leg of their journey.

Chapter 10: Paths Aligned

The day had dawned over a shattered horizon—a sky smeared with the bruised hues of early twilight that promised both despair and the glimmer of renewal. Ryo and Kota had journeyed far from the remnants of the Mirage Village and the haunted corridors of the ruined city. Now, they found themselves at the edge of an endless plain where the very fabric of time seemed to be thinning. Here, the fractured remnants of history, the present decay, and the whispers of a hopeful future converged in a fragile, trembling equilibrium. The plain was a vast, desolate area of cracked earth and scattered rubble.

Occasional patches of resilient green poked through the parched soil—a defiant reminder that even in the harshest conditions, life stubbornly persisted. At the centre of this barren land, a distant glow beckoned like a beacon, its light pulsating with an otherworldly rhythm. Ryo had heard the old legends spoken in hushed tones by survivors: that there would come a moment when the scattered shards of time would align, when the lost moments of the past would converge with the promise of tomorrow. That moment, he now realized with mounting certainty, had arrived. Ryo stood at the cliff of a low ridge that overlooked the plain. Below him, the ground was etched with deep fissures, each one a scar of the disaster that had torn the world apart. In the distance, the sky shimmered with strange distortions—rifts that pulsed with erratic energy. The boundaries of the circle were indistinct, as though the very air was bending around it, distorting the world outside its luminous core. Within the circle, the landscape seemed to shimmer with a surreal calm.

The turbulent energies of the rifts, so fierce just moments before, were drawn into a singular rhythm—a slow, steady cadence that made Ryo's skin prickle with both awe and foreboding.

"Kota," he murmured, kneeling on the cool stone,

"this is it. The convergence... it's happening."

Kota's dark eyes met Ryo's with a calm intensity that belied the turmoil around them. The faithful dog shifted his weight and trotted to Ryo's side, as if ready to lead the way into the unknown. Ryo retrieved from his pack the small blue shard he'd collected in the ruins—a fragment of light that pulsed in time with his own heartbeat. He held it high for a moment, watching as its glow merged with the ambient light of the plain. At that instant, the shard's soft radiance seemed to resonate with a deeper frequency, harmonizing with the distant hum that vibrated beneath the surface of the earth.

The very air around them trembled, as if the threads of time were straining against one another in anticipation. A low, resonant hum swelled into a chorus of sound—a symphony of overlapping voices, the echoes of the past mingling with tentative notes of the future.

Ryo's heart raced as he took in the sight: the fissures in the earth began to glow with a pale, ethereal light, and ghostly images danced at the edge of his vision. In one fleeting moment, he saw a memory of a bustling street from decades before; in another, he glimpsed a possible future where the ruins were replaced by gleaming spires and verdant parks. These images flashed by in a disjointed montage—a kaleidoscope of possibility and loss. Every step toward the centre of the convergence felt like an act of defiance against the relentless chaos of fractured time.

Ryo moved slowly at first, each step measured and laden with a mix of dread and hope. The ground beneath him vibrated with a subtle pulse—like the beating of an enormous, ancient heart—and as he ascended the final slope, the convergence came into clearer focus.

As he stepped forward, the ground under his feet pulsed in synchrony with the beat of his heart. The air grew thick with the scent of ozone and the faint aroma of something ancient and powerful. For a moment, time itself appeared to pause—each second stretching into eternity. Ryo closed his eyes and listened; in that suspended moment, he could almost hear the whispers of those who had come before, their voices carried on the wind like fragments of forgotten dreams.

When he opened his eyes, the convergence circle shone with a brilliant light. Within it, shapes and shadows coalesced—a swirling tapestry of events not yet written and memories long past. In that surreal illustration, Ryo saw the faces of those he had lost, glimpses of a future where hope might be reborn, and—most strikingly— the unwavering image of Kota, radiating a warmth and power that defied explanation. It was as if the dog's very essence was the keystone holding the fractured moments together. Ryo's mind reeled with the implications.

Now, standing at the nexus of converging time, he understood with painful clarity that Kota was more than a companion; he was the Timekeeper's Heart—a living embodiment of hope and order in a chaotic, broken timeline. The ground trembled again, and the luminous circle pulsed with renewed intensity.

The rifts around the convergence seemed to align, their chaotic energies drawn into a single, potent current. It was a breathtaking moment, a fragile peace amid the raw power of the cosmos. Ryo's breath caught in his throat as he extended a trembling hand toward Kota, who stepped forward, eyes shining with an inner light. In that silent communion, Ryo felt an unspoken promise pass between them—a vow to protect, to endure, and to strive for a future where the wounds of the past might one day be healed.

The air shimmered as the convergence reached its zenith. The boundaries between past, present, and future blurred into one continuous moment, a singular pulse of existence that reverberated through every living thing. Ryo's vision filled with a cascade of images: the sounds of children in a long-forgotten park, the quiet determination of a lover's farewell, the hopeful glimmer of a sunrise over a city reborn.

These visions were both a blessing and a burden—a reminder of what had been lost and what could be salvaged if the fractured threads of time could be mended.

A deep, resonant voice seemed to rise from the very earth beneath him—a voice that spoke not in words, but in the language of pulses and vibrations. It carried the weight of ages and the promise of renewal. Ryo listened, his eyes fixed on the swirling vortex of light. In that moment, he knew that the convergence was not an end but a beginning—a threshold through which the future might be reclaimed if one had the courage to step forward. Kota barked softly, a sound that cut through the silence and anchored Ryo to the present.

The dog's steadfast presence was a lifeline amid the overwhelming tide of possibility.

"We're not done yet," Ryo murmured, more to himself than to Kota.

"There's so much more to do. I have to believe that from these shattered pieces, we can rebuild something new." As the brilliant light of the convergence slowly receded, the landscape around Ryo began to reassert its familiar form— ruined buildings, cracked roads, and the ever-present scars of a world marred by chaos. Yet everything had changed subtly.

The oppressive tension that had once filled the air was replaced by a tentative calm, as if the world were taking a deep, collective breath. The rifts, though still visible in the distance, pulsed in a more measured rhythm—one that hinted at a potential healing of the fractured timeline.

Ryo stood for a long moment, absorbing the magnitude of what had just transpired. The convergence had been a fleeting glimpse of what might be—a promise of a future where the past's wounds could be healed.

But it was also a stark reminder of the challenges that lay ahead. The dark forces that had exploited time were still out there, lurking in the shadows, waiting for their chance to plunge the world back into chaos. With a deep, steadying breath, Ryo turned toward the path that led back into the ruins.

"We have to move forward," he said softly, his voice resolute.

"The convergence has shown us what might be possible—but it's up to us to make it a reality."

Kota bounded at his side, the determination in his eyes echoing the unspoken promise that had been forged in the heart of the convergence. Together, they began their descent from the plateau, leaving behind the awe-inspiring spectacle of converging time for the uncertain path ahead. As they retraced their steps through the fractured landscape, Ryo's mind churned with plans and questions. How could he harness the fragile calm that the convergence had granted?

What did it mean for the dark forces that still hunted them? And, most pressingly, how could he protect Kota—his Timekeeper's Heart—from those who would seek to exploit his power for nefarious ends? Every step along the way was measured, every moment a reminder that time was both a relentless enemy and a fragile ally.

The visions of the convergence had imprinted themselves upon Ryo's soul, igniting a spark of hope that burned bright even in the darkest hours. He knew that the journey ahead would be fraught with peril, but that very peril was the crucible in which a new future might be forged. The first light of dawn broke on the horizon as

Ryo and Kota neared the outskirts of a familiar ruin—a crumbling city block that once buzzed with life. In the soft glow of the morning, Ryo could see subtle signs of change: a broken window glinted as if newly repaired, a faded mural on a wall seemed to glow with an inner light, and even the rusted remains of a car, half-buried in debris, held a spark of vibrancy.

It was as though the convergence had sown the seeds of renewal among the scars of the past. Ryo paused at the edge of the block and knelt beside Kota.

"Look at this," he said, his voice filled with both wonder and determination.

"It's as if time itself is healing these wounds, one small piece at a time." Kota licked his hand, a silent affirmation that, despite the weight of the world, there was still beauty—and hope—to be found. In that quiet moment, Ryo resolved to carry the promise of the convergence with him, to let its memory guide his actions as he ventured deeper into the uncertain future.

The convergence had been a brief, brilliant burst of clarity—a reminder that even in a world shattered by chaos, the threads of time could be mended if one had the courage to weave them. As Ryo and Kota continued on their journey, the landscape around them gradually assumed a new character. The once-violent distortions in the air had softened to a gentle shimmer, like heat haze on a hot day, and the oppressive weight of the past had given way to a tentative optimism.

Though danger still lurked in the shadows and the dark forces that had fractured time were not yet vanquished, Ryo felt a stirring of hope—a belief that the future was not a predetermined fate but a canvas upon which new possibilities could be painted. With each step, the memory of the convergence burned brightly in his mind—a vivid reminder of what could be achieved if he remained true to the promise he had made to himself and to Kota.

"We'll keep moving," he murmured, glancing down at his faithful companion.

"No matter what comes next, we'll build a new tomorrow from the ruins of today." And so, with the pale light of dawn illuminating the battered yet resilient world, Ryo and Kota pressed forward into the uncertain horizon. Their journey had entered a new phase—a phase defined not by the relentless march of destruction, but by the delicate interplay of loss and hope, of despair and the enduring spark of possibility. The convergence had passed, but its echoes would guide them as they strove to reclaim a future that was still worth fighting for. In that final, quiet moment before the sun climbed higher into the sky, Ryo looked out over the horizon, his eyes fixed on the endless area of possibility.

The future was uncertain, but in that moment, it shimmered with promise—a promise that, even in the fractured tapestry of time, the human spirit could weave a new destiny.

Chapter 11: Hollow Light

Ryo and Kota found themselves drawn toward a place whispered about among the survivors—a forest where time did not merely pass but echoed. Tales of this forest had circulated like urban legend: a place where memories materialized in the rustling leaves and ghostly voices drifted on the wind. For Ryo, already burdened with the revelations of Kota's extraordinary nature, the promise of answers—however cryptic—was irresistible.

They reached the forest's edge as dusk began to melt into night. A dense canopy of ancient trees rose before them, their gnarled branches interlocking high overhead to form a vaulted ceiling of dark leaves. The forest was alive with sound: not the conventional chorus of nocturnal creatures, but a layered symphony of murmurs—whispers that seemed both distant and intimately close, as if the voices of forgotten souls were conversing in a language older than time. Ryo paused at the threshold, his breath catching as he surveyed the scene.

"This must be it, Kota," he murmured, his voice barely audible. The dog, sensing the significance of the place, sat quietly by his side, his dark eyes reflecting the soft, spectral light that filtered through the leaves. Together, they stepped into the forest. The transition was almost seamless—a shift from the harsh, cracked vistas of the Wastes to a realm that pulsed with a mysterious, gentle rhythm. The forest floor was carpeted with soft moss and fallen leaves, and the air, though cool and damp, was injected with an indefinable energy that prickled at Ryo's skin.

As they ventured deeper, the sounds of the forest grew more insistent. Faint, indistinct voices echoed among the trees—a racket of whispers that could easily be mistaken for the wind. Yet, as Ryo listened more intently, he began to distinguish words, syllables, and even fragments of conversations.

They were as if the forest itself was remembering: recollections of long-gone days, voices of people who had once walked these lands, and even hints of futures that might have been. Ryo's mind wandered to the vision he had experienced with the shard. The images of a bustling, hopeful city, children playing, and the quiet joy of simple moments now seemed to resonate with the murmurs around him.

"These are memories," he whispered, more to himself than to Kota.

"The forest... it holds echoes of what was and what might have been."

The deeper they walked, the more surreal the surroundings became. Trees, centuries old, arched overhead like ancient sentinels. Their bark was etched with patterns that looked almost like symbols—a language of nature, conveying secrets of the earth and the passage of time. In one clearing, Ryo discovered a fallen log covered in luminous fungi.

The soft, ethereal light it emitted bathed the clearing in a dreamlike glow, and for a moment, he swore he saw shapes moving in the perimeter of his vision—fleeting spirits that vanished when he tried to focus on them.

Kota led the way with steady determination, occasionally pausing as if to listen for something only he could hear. At one point, the dog darted toward a copse of trees and began barking softly, tail wagging with a mixture of curiosity and insistence. Ryo hurried to catch up and found Kota fixated on a narrow gap between two massive trunks. Beyond the gap, a soft, golden light filtered in, and Ryo's heart skipped a beat.

The light was warm and inviting—a stark contrast to the cool shadows of the surrounding forest. It beckoned him closer, promising a revelation hidden in its radiance.

Drawing near, Ryo discovered that the gap opened into a small valley, a secluded clearing where time appeared to slow. Here, the air was filled with the scent of pine and fresh rain, though no rain had fallen in what felt like ages. In the centre of the valley stood a weathered stone pedestal covered in moss and lichen.

Resting on top of the pedestal was a delicate hourglass, its glass remarkably intact, though filled not with sand but with a fine, glowing dust that shimmered in the dim light. The hourglass turned slowly, as if moved by an unseen hand, marking the passage of time in a steady, hypnotic rhythm. Ryo approached it slowly, his steps measured. Every fibre of his being trembled with a mix of awe and fear.

He recalled the ancient texts he had seen in the ruined library—the cryptic inscriptions that spoke of "living time" and the possibility that time itself could be anchored by powerful relics. Could this hourglass be one of those relics? And if so, what did it mean for him and for Kota—the Timekeeper's Heart? He reached out and brushed his fingers lightly along the cool surface of the pedestal. For a heartbeat, the forest was silent, the myriad echoes of voices pausing as if waiting for his touch. Then, as if in response, the hourglass began to glow faintly.

The dust within shimmered, and the gentle ticking sound grew louder, merging with the ambient whispers of the forest. A sudden gust of wind swept through the valley, stirring the dust and causing the hourglass to spin more rapidly. Ryo staggered back, shielding his eyes as the light intensified. In that moment, the forest around him seemed to pulsate with memories

He saw flashes of a time long past—a family gathered around a table filled with food, children running through a sunlit meadow, elders telling stories beneath the canopy of ancient trees. The images were fleeting, disjointed, yet each carried a potent sense of joy and loss. Kota barked, drawing Ryo's attention. The dog had moved to the base of a nearby oak, where an inscription had been carved deep into the bark. The inscription, though weathered, was still legible— a series of symbols interwoven with words in an ancient tongue that Ryo could not decipher.

Yet, despite his inability to understand it, he felt that it was significant—perhaps a key to unlocking the mysteries of the hourglass and, by extension, the nature of time itself.

Ryo knelt beside the oak, tracing the symbols with his fingertips. In the act of touching the ancient carving, he felt a subtle vibration beneath his skin—a connection, as if the tree itself was alive with the memory of centuries.

The forest around him seemed to lean in, as though urging him to decipher its secrets. The hourglass's glow pulsed together with his heartbeat, a steady reminder that time, though fractured, still beat on.

As minutes stretched into what felt like hours, Ryo's initial awe transformed into a deep, introspective contemplation.

The valley with its serene beauty and visible sense of history, offered a rare moment of clarity amid the chaos of his journey. Here, he realized, lay the echoes of tomorrow—the lingering hopes and memories of a world that could be, if only one had the courage to reclaim it from the ashes of the past. In the quiet of that timeless valley, Ryo sat cross-legged on the soft grass, Kota curled up at his feet.

He produced a small, battered notebook from his pack and began to write, capturing every detail of the moment—the glow of the hourglass, the inscriptions on the oak, the soft murmur of voices that floated on the breeze. He wrote of the family he'd glimpsed in his vision, the conversations and sorrow intermingled in those fleeting images, and the profound sense that every memory was a stepping stone toward a better tomorrow.

The forest, as if in response to his quiet resolve, seemed to share its secrets. The gentle rustling of leaves transformed into a chorus of soft, overlapping voices—a symphony of memories that transcended time. Ryo closed his eyes and listened, letting the voices wash over him. They were not the voices of the living, but echoes of those who had once walked these lands, of hopes that had blossomed and withered under the relentless march of time.

For a long while, he sat there in the glow of the hourglass, absorbing the lessons of the forest. He realized that the Echoing Forest was not merely a repository of old memories, but a living archive of what the world had once been—and what it might become again. Each whisper, each flicker of light, was a reminder that time was not lost forever; it was waiting to be reclaimed by those brave enough to remember.

Kota stirred and lifted his head, his eyes fixed on the far edge of the valley where the forest thickened into darkness. Ryo sensed that his faithful companion, too, felt the pull of the unknown—a call to venture further into the heart of the forest where answers might lie hidden among the ancient trees. Reluctantly, Ryo closed his notebook and stood, casting one last, lingering glance at the hourglass and the oak's inscription.

"We have a way to go, Kota," he said softly, his voice resolute yet tinged with melancholy.

"There's more to these echoes than I can understand here. We must follow them—find out what happened, and perhaps, what can still be." Together, Ryo and Kota stepped away from the glen, the soft hum of the forest's memories accompanying them as they left the sanctuary of the Echoing Forest behind. The forest's ancient voices faded into the background, but their resonance remained in Ryo's heart—a constant reminder of the power of memory and the promise of tomorrow.

Outside the valley, the forest grew denser, the trees standing close together as if guarding secrets that only the brave dared uncover. The path ahead was uncertain, twisting through narrow corridors of intertwined branches and shadows. Every step was accompanied by the rustle of leaves and the distant echo of laughs and sorrow—a silent testimony to the lives that had once flourished in these woods.

Ryo's mind churned with questions as they advanced: What secrets did the forest hold? Could the ancient inscriptions and the hourglass be pieces of a larger puzzle—a map to reclaiming the fractured timeline? And what role would Kota, the living Timekeeper's Heart, play in restoring the balance of a world lost to chaos? As night fell, the forest transformed once more. The darkness was not oppressive here but filled with a mysterious luminescence. Bioluminescent fungi clung to the tree trunks, casting an eerie, otherworldly glow that lit their path in soft blues and greens.

Shadows danced among the undergrowth, and every so often, Ryo caught sight of a flicker—a face, a hand, a memory—that vanished as quickly as it appeared.

They paused beside a small stream that trickled through the forest floor, its clear water reflecting the shifting light of the glowing fungi. Ryo knelt to drink, and as the cool water touched his lips, he felt a profound connection to the forest's timeless spirit. The murmuring brook, the rustling leaves, and even Kota's soft panting merged into a single, soothing rhythm—a lullaby of memories that spoke of resilience, loss, and the enduring possibility of renewal.

Ryo knew that the journey through the Echoing Forest was just one step on a long road. Ahead lay more dangers and more mysteries: the dark forces that sought to exploit the fractured time, the elusive knowledge hidden in the ruins of the old world, and the ever-present burden of destiny that now rested on his shoulders. Yet, in that moment, amid the gentle glow and the soft echoes of a thousand voices, he felt a spark of hope. It was a fragile light, yet one that refused to be extinguished.

As the first hints of dawn began to pierce the horizon, Ryo and Kota emerged from the depths of the forest. The cool, dewy air of early morning greeted them, and the distant sounds of a waking world stirred in the background. Though the Echoing Forest receded behind them like a half-remembered dream, its lessons were etched into their souls. Ryo clutched his notebook close to his heart, determined to unravel the secrets of those ancient echoes and to use them as a guide on his journey to mend a shattered timeline.

"Every memory counts," Ryo murmured as they stepped onto a narrow road leading out of the forest.

"Every echo, every whisper—they're all pieces of a puzzle. And we're going to put it together, no matter what." Kota responded with a soft bark, his eyes reflecting a steadfast loyalty and an inner strength that gave Ryo hope.

The road ahead was uncertain, winding through the broken remnants of a world that had long since forgotten what it meant to dream. Yet, as long as the echoes of the forest lived on in their hearts, there remained a promise of a new tomorrow—a tomorrow that they would forge from the fragments of a lost past.

With the rising sun casting golden hues over the horizon, Ryo and Kota continued their journey, the gentle resonance of the Echoing Forest still echoing in their minds. Each step they took was a defiant act of hope—a promise that even in a world fractured by time, the bonds of memory and love could guide them toward a future worth reclaiming.

Chapter 12: Keeper's Path

The chill of early morning had barely begun to lift when Ryo and Kota emerged from the echoing quiet of the forest. The night's lessons— the whispered memories of the Echoing Forest— still lingered in Ryo's mind, each echo a reminder of a time long past and a promise of what might yet be reclaimed.

Today, the road ahead seemed to shimmer with possibility, as though the fractured strands of time were gradually converging toward something new. Ryo's boots crunched over debris along a half-forgotten path that wound between crumbling stone walls and overgrown ruins. His eyes, though tired, glowed with determination as he recalled Kaori's parting words beneath the collapsed overpass:

"Trust the bond you share with him." He had clung to those words ever since, watching in awe as Kota—the quiet, steadfast force—had tamed chaotic rifts and calmed the raging winds of fractured time. Now, with the lessons of the Mirage Village and the Echoing Forest fresh in his heart, Ryo felt that the next phase of his journey was about to begin. As the path meandered toward the outskirts of what was once a thriving quarter of the old city, a soft, almost musical hum began to resonate in the air. It was subtle at first, a background vibration beneath the normal clamour of the ruined world, but it grew steadily in volume and clarity. Ryo stopped on a raised patch of ground—a remnant of a once-grand plaza—and closed his eyes.

In the silence of his heart, he listened to the vibration, trying to understand its meaning. It was as if the very earth was speaking a language older than memory itself.

"Kota," he murmured, kneeling to stroke the dog's fur,

"do you feel it? It's as if the ground is alive with its own rhythm." Kota's ears twitched and his gaze sharpened. The dog stepped forward as if drawn by an unseen call, and Ryo followed. The path led them to a crumbling archway adorned with fading murals and intricate carvings—a remnant of the city's past glory. Here, the hum became a low, steady pulse that vibrated beneath Ryo's feet. It was in this place, he sensed, that the fractured threads of time began to weave themselves into something coherent.

A figure emerged from the shadows beneath the arch. It was Kaori, the mysterious woman who had once warned him beneath the collapsed overpass. Her dark cloak blended with the early morning gloom, and her golden eyes shone with a certainty that belied the weariness in her face. Ryo's heart skipped a beat. He had long hoped to see her again.

"Ryo," Kaori said, her voice soothing.

"I have been waiting for you on this path." Ryo rose, his hand instinctively drifting toward the hilt of his knife, but the warmth in Kaori's gaze soon eased his tension.

"Kaori... what is it you wish to show me?" he asked, trying to steady his voice.

"Last time we met, you spoke of a destiny intertwined with Kota's power—a secret of time itself. I need to understand." Kaori stepped closer, her eyes never leaving Ryo's.

"There is a path—a way to mend the fractures that have torn this world apart. But it lies beyond what you have seen so far. You must follow your intuition with Kota and follow the signs laid out by time's own hand." She extended a hand, and with a small, knowing smile, she gestured to the ancient archway behind them.

"This place was built as a gateway, a portal of sorts to the wisdom of the old world. The artisans and scholars of that era believed that time was not a straight line but a tapestry woven of countless threads. Some of these threads—if one were wise enough—could be plucked and guided to mend the broken whole." Ryo listened intently, his eyes widening as Kaori's words began to resonate with all that he had witnessed in recent days—the strange calm of Kota amid chaotic rifts, the timeless echoes of the forest, the visions in the shard.

"Are you saying that… that Kota is not merely a loyal companion? That he is part of a greater force?" he asked quietly. Kaori nodded.

"Yes. You have come to know him as the Timekeeper's Heart—a living embodiment of time's steady pulse amid the chaos. His presence creates a resonance that can align fractured moments, even if only for brief instants. But this power is not unlimited. It is a spark that must be nurtured, a light that you must protect if you hope to use it to restore balance."

The wind picked up around them, stirring the fallen leaves and carrying with it the faint murmur of voices—echoes of a time when the world was whole. Ryo felt the air thicken with possibility, as if the very fabric of existence was readying itself for something momentous.

"Show me the way, Kaori," Ryo said, his voice resolute despite the uncertainty in his heart.

"I want to understand how to harness this power—to mend what has been broken." Kaori smiled gently, a bittersweet expression of both hope and sorrow.

"The path is not an easy one. It is fraught with peril, and the constant threat of those who would seek to exploit this power for their own ends. But if you are willing to walk it, if you can draw strength from the bond you share with Kota, then you may yet change the course of time."

She led them deeper along the path, away from the crumbling archway and into a corridor flanked by ancient stone pillars covered in moss and faded inscriptions.

Each pillar bore symbols that Ryo could not decipher—a language of the past that spoke of cycles, renewal, and the eternal flow of time.

The hum grew louder here, its rhythm syncing with Ryo's heartbeat as if welcoming him into a sacred space. As they walked, Kaori explained, "In the old texts, they spoke of the Timekeeper's Path—a journey that one must undertake to reclaim lost time and restore balance. It is not just a physical journey through ruins and forgotten places, but a quest for understanding the very essence of existence. The key lies in embracing the memories of yesterday, the hopes of tomorrow, and the love that binds the present. That is what you and Kota represent—a union of past, present, and future."

Ryo's eyes glistened as he absorbed her words. Every hardship, every moment of doubt, suddenly seemed to converge into a single purpose.

"I've seen fragments of what might have been," he confessed, his voice trembling with a mix of emotion and resolve.

"I've seen the echoes of a future where the world is whole again. And I know now that those echoes are not mere dreams—they are warnings, and perhaps, directions." Kaori's expression softened further.

"You must learn to read those echoes, Ryo. They are the whispers of time, guiding you to the hidden knowledge of the past. In the ruins of ancient libraries, in the faded murals on forgotten walls, in the quiet places where nature reclaims what once was, there lie clues to what can be restored. But you must also listen to the bond between you and Kota. His instincts, his unwavering presence—these are gifts that have been bestowed upon you both."

They reached a clearing where the ancient pillars gave way to a small courtyard. In the centre of the courtyard stood a stone basin, its surface engraved with intricate patterns. Water trickled from a broken spout, creating a soft murmur that blended with the distant hum of the world. Kaori motioned for Ryo to approach the basin.

"Place your hand upon the stone," she instructed.

"Let the memory of this place, and the energy of the Timekeeper's Heart, flow into you." With hesitant determination, Ryo knelt before the basin and rested his palm on the cool, rough stone. In that instant, a surge of sensation flooded him—a mixture of warmth, sorrow, and hope that seemed to carry the collective memories of the lost world. He closed his eyes and felt images and emotions swirl behind his eyelids: flashes of long-forgotten celebrations, the conversations of children, and the quiet determination of those who had fought to preserve a world now reduced to ruins.

Among these, the steady presence of Kota shone like a beacon—a reminder of the enduring power of loyalty and love. When Ryo opened his eyes, Kaori was watching him with gentle intensity.

"The path is open to you," she said quietly.

"But remember: the power you feel now is fragile. It must be nurtured with understanding and protected with sacrifice. The choices you make from this moment on will shape not only your destiny but that of all time." Ryo slowly withdrew his hand from the stone, feeling both exhilarated and burdened by the revelation.

"I understand," he murmured.

"I must learn to honour the bond I share with Kota and use it to guide me. I must reclaim the fragments of time that have been scattered, and perhaps, piece together a future that can mend the past." Kaori nodded, her eyes reflecting a depth of sorrow and hope that resonated with the ancient stones around them.

"There is much to do, Ryo. The Timekeeper's

path is not a single road but a network of trials—each one a test of your resolve, your compassion, and your willingness to confront the darkness that seeks to consume the light. You must seek out the remnants of the old world, listen to the echoes in the forgotten places, and never lose sight of what truly matters." For a long moment, the only sound was the soft lapping of water in the basin and the distant, steady hum of the converging rifts in the world beyond.

Ryo felt that he stood at the threshold of a great journey—a pilgrimage into the heart of time itself. The weight of destiny pressed upon him, yet it was tempered by the comforting presence of Kota at his side. The dog's steady, unassuming loyalty was a constant amid the shifting tides of fate.

"Thank you, Kaori," Ryo said softly, his voice filled with both gratitude and determination.

"I will follow this path. I will learn from the past and build a future that honours everything we've lost—and everything we still have." Kaori offered him a small, bittersweet smile.

"Then go, Ryo. The Timekeeper's Path awaits. Remember, every step you take, every memory you reclaim, will serve as a light in the darkness. Follow your intuition with Kota, and let it be the beacon that guides you through even the deepest shadows."

With that, Kaori stepped back into the lingering twilight, her figure slowly dissolving into the mists that clung to the ancient ruins. Ryo stared after her until she vanished completely, then turned his attention to the path ahead. He gathered his few belongings and rose to his feet, glancing down at Kota, whose eyes shone with unwavering trust. Together, they resumed their journey along the winding road that would lead them deeper into the heart of the ruined city—and perhaps, into the long-forgotten sanctuaries of the old world where the secrets of time lay hidden. Every step was filled with a renewed sense of purpose.

The revelations at the stone basin had ignited within Ryo a fierce determination to protect the fragile power within Kota—the very power that might one day restore order to the fractured timeline. As they walked, the landscape around them began to transform. The barren roads gave way to overgrown gardens where wildflowers pushed through cracks in the pavement, and the ruins of old buildings were slowly being reclaimed by nature. It was as if the earth itself was beginning to heal—a subtle, hopeful sign amid the lingering scars of the Time Rapture.

Ryo's mind was an uproar of plans and possibilities. He resolved to seek out ancient archives, forgotten libraries, and secret meeting places of survivors who might hold clues to the mysteries of the past. Each relic of history was a piece of the grand puzzle—a puzzle that, when assembled, might reveal how to mend the broken fabric of time. And through it all, he would keep the truth of Kota's power close to his heart, nurturing it as the precious spark that it was. The journey along the Timekeeper's Path was not without its challenges.

As Ryo and Kota moved through corridors of crumbling stone and tangled roots, they encountered other traveller's—some weary and resigned, others defiant in the face of despair. In quiet, whispered conversations, these fellow wanderers spoke of legends and omens, of visions that had guided them through the darkness.

Each shared story added to the mosaic of hope that Ryo was slowly piecing together, a tapestry woven from the memories of those who had come before and the promise of those who still believed in the possibility of renewal.

At one point, while resting by a small stream that cut through the ruins like a silver ribbon, Ryo encountered an old man draped in tattered robes. The man's eyes were bright despite the hardship etched into every line of his face.

"You carry a great light, young man," the old man said in a low, measured tone.

"That light, in the form of your loyal companion, is more than a mere beacon—it is the pulse of time. Guard it well, and it will guide you to what you seek." Ryo nodded slowly, the old man's words resonating deeply with his recent revelations.

"I will," he promised, his voice barely above a whisper.

"I will protect him, and I will protect the hope that he represents." As dusk fell once more, Ryo and Kota found shelter in the ruins of an old courtyard. Under a sky streaked with the deep purples and golds of the setting sun, Ryo sat with his notebook open, scribbling down everything he had learned that day—every symbol on the ancient pillars, every whispered word from the wind, every flicker of light that danced around him in moments of revelation.

The pages filled quickly with sketches and notes, forming the beginnings of a guide—a record of the Timekeeper's Path that might one day be shared with others desperate to reclaim the fractured future. Kota lay at his feet, occasionally lifting his head as if to listen to the nocturnal symphony of the crumbling world.

This bond—between man and dog, between past and future—was the cornerstone of his resolve. It was a promise that even in a world where time itself had been torn apart, hope could still be nurtured, and destiny could still be reclaimed. In the gentle embrace of twilight, as the first stars began to twinkle in the recovering sky, Ryo closed his notebook and whispered to the silent night,

"Tomorrow, we continue. Tomorrow, we follow the Timekeeper's Path." The words, though soft, carried the weight of a promise—a promise to walk bravely into the unknown, guided by the enduring light of memory and the timeless bond with Kota. And so, with the chill of night settling over the ruins and the distant hum of time's pulse echoing in his ears, Ryo drifted into a fitful sleep, the gentle rhythm of his heartbeat mingling with the quiet murmur of the old stones around him.

Chapter 13: The Unraveling

The wasteland had grown even more treacherous since Ryo and Kota last set out from the ruins. With every step, the landscape seemed to twist as if the very fabric of time itself were on the verge of unraveling further. Ryo's mind was still reeling from the revelations of the Timekeeper's Heart—a truth that had set his heart ablaze with both hope and dread. Now, however, a similar threat was closing in. They had been traveling along a narrow, winding road that cut between jagged rock outcrops and clusters of skeletal trees when a low, resonant hum began to vibrate in the air.

The sound, unlike the usual distant rumbles of unstable rifts or the whistling wind, carried a purposeful cadence. Ryo's eyes narrowed as he listened. Kota's ears, ever alert, pricked forward, and his body stiffened as if bracing for an unseen blow. Before Ryo could voice his concern, figures emerged from behind a copse of dead trees.

Clad in patchwork armour of scavenged metal and dark cloth, these individuals moved with the silent precision of predators. Their eyes glinted with calculated malice, and at their centre strode a tall figure with a face obscured by a hood and a mask fashioned from twisted metal scraps. This was no random band of scavengers—these were the Rift Hunters, a notorious faction rumoured to manipulate the very currents of time for their own benefit.

"Hold!" the leader commanded in a low, chilling voice that cut through the still air.

"You there, stop!" Ryo froze, his heart pounding in his ears. He slowly raised a hand in a gesture of non-aggression, though his grip tightened around the makeshift spear at his side. Kota, ever protective, placed himself slightly in front of Ryo, growling softly. The masked leader stepped forward, his gaze shifting between Ryo and the loyal dog.

"You've been on the move for too long, wanderer," he said, his tone both mocking and dangerous.

"And that creature by your side... it sings to the rifts. It pulses with a power that we have been seeking." Ryo's stomach churned.

"I'm not interested in trading my companion," he said, voice steady despite the fear knotting inside him.

"We're simply trying to survive." A cold laugh erupted from the leader.

"Survival is for the weak," he sneered.

"But you—your dog is special. It is, as the legends say, the Timekeeper's Heart. We intend to harness that power to reshape what remains of this broken world. Surrender him to us, and perhaps we will spare you." At those words, Ryo's blood ran cold. He had suspected that word of

Kota's uncanny abilities had spread, but he had never imagined that these Hunters would come so boldly to claim him.

"You'll have to take me first," Ryo replied, his voice hardening.

"I won't let you exploit him." Without warning, the ambush erupted. Two of the Hunters lunged toward Ryo, their crude weapons raised. Ryo dodged a swinging club, parrying with his spear as he spun to meet the attack. Kota, sensing the peril, leapt forward with a fierce bark and bit at one of the assailants' arms, forcing the man to cry out and recoil in pain. Chaos exploded in a flurry of movement. Ryo's training—and sheer desperation—took over. He thrust his spear with precision, knocking one attacker off balance. Yet there were many, and their coordinated strikes pressed in from multiple sides. Their leader, still cloaked in shadow, circled around with predatory calm, his eyes fixed on Kota.

"Hand over the dog!" the masked man shouted, his voice echoing with cruel authority.

"Or perish with him!" Ryo's heart pounded as he fought off another blow. He swung his spear in a wide arc, sending an assailant sprawling into the rubble. But even as he repelled their initial assault, he knew that this was only the beginning—a meticulously laid trap designed not merely to capture him, but to take Kota from his grasp by force if necessary. Time seemed to slow as Ryo caught sight of something extraordinary. Amid the pandemonium of battle, he saw that every time Kota moved, a subtle change rippled through the chaotic energy of the nearby rift—a rift that pulsed violently in the distance. Wherever Kota stepped, the distorted air stilled, as if the creature's very presence commanded a momentary order out of chaos. Ryo's eyes widened in realization: his loyal companion was not just an innocent pet; he was a living channel of temporal power—a beacon in the fractured chain.

"Stay with me, Kota!" Ryo roared, ducking under a sweeping blow. He knew that if the Hunters succeeded, they would not only capture Kota but also unleash forces that could further destabilize the already fragile timeline.

With renewed determination, Ryo advanced, his movements a blend of calculated skill and raw, protective fury. He parried another strike and lunged forward, driving his spear deep into the shoulder of an attacker.

The man cried out, collapsing into a pile of debris. Kota, ever fearless, bounded toward another foe who had crept close from behind, teeth sinking into the man's leg with a snarl that vibrated with fierce loyalty.

The battle raged on for what felt like endless minutes, each second stretching into a vortex of adrenaline and chaos. The masked leader's voice cut through the uproar repeatedly, his commands laced with a venom that chilled Ryo's blood.

"Surrender the Timekeeper's Heart! You have no idea the power you hold!" At one point, as Ryo struggled to fend off a particularly determined attack from two Hunters, he saw an opportunity. The rift behind them flared with a sudden burst of unstable energy—a chaotic flash of light that disoriented friend and foe alike.

In that moment of disarray, Ryo grabbed Kota and bolted for cover, weaving through the shattered remains of a collapsed wall and ducking behind a mass of twisted metal. They crouched in the shadow of the debris, hearts pounding, as the sounds of clashing steel and anguished shouts faded into a distant din.

Ryo pressed his back against the cool surface, his eyes scanning the area for any sign of pursuit. Kota's fur bristled; the dog was tense and alert, every muscle coiled in readiness. A low voice came from the darkness.

"You cannot hide forever, Ryo." The masked leader's tone was almost conversational now, as though he regarded this confrontation as merely a prelude to something far more significant.

Ryo's jaw tightened.

"I will never give you Kota," he spat.

"He's more than just a means to an end." The voice chuckled softly.

"Ah, but you see, that is where you're mistaken. In him lies a power that can alter the course of fate—a power that we have long coveted. You are merely delaying the inevitable."

For a long, agonizing moment, silence reigned. Then, as if in response to Ryo's unyielding defiance, the ground beneath them trembled—a reminder of the unstable rift that loomed ominously in the distance.

The air filled with a visible energy, and in that charged silence, Ryo felt the weight of destiny pressing down on him. His mind raced with a single, undeniable truth: if the Hunters succeeded in capturing Kota, the fragile balance of time would shatter beyond repair. Gathering every ounce of resolve, Ryo rose from his hiding place.

"If you want him, you'll have to come through me!" he roared, his voice echoing across the ruined landscape. With Kota at his side, Ryo charged from behind the debris, spear held high. The sudden movement startled the remaining Rift Hunters, and in that brief moment of confusion, Ryo managed to drive a powerful thrust toward the masked leader.

The leader staggered, a snarl of pain contorting his features.

"You fool!" he hissed, rallying his men with renewed ferocity. But the battle had shifted. The Hunters, caught off-guard by Ryo's sudden surge, faltered in their coordination. Ryo seized the opportunity, parrying blows and retaliating with fierce strikes. Kota, ever the embodiment of loyalty and hidden power, fought alongside him with a ferocity that defied his small stature—teeth snapping, claws raking, each movement a testament to the living miracle he was. In the midst of the renewed onslaught, the unstable rift behind them flared again.

Its turbulent energies cascaded over the battlefield, bathing the combatants in a surreal light. For a split second, the chaos of battle was suspended in a haunting image: Time itself seemed to hold its breath as the rift pulsed, and for that moment, Ryo could swear he saw visions of another world—a vision of hope, of a future rebuilt from the ashes of the past. But as quickly as it had come, the vision faded, and the battle resumed with renewed intensity.

Ryo's muscles burned and his vision blurred with sweat, but his determination did not waver. With every strike, every parry, he sent a clear message to the Hunters: he would protect Kota, the Timekeeper's Heart, no matter the cost.

The masked leader, bleeding and enraged, gave one final command, his voice trembling with fury.

"Retreat! Regroup and return—if you value your lives, you will surrender the dog to us!" The Ruthless Faction, their numbers diminished by Ryo's relentless assault, began to withdraw into the darkened corridors of the ruined city. Their retreat was not an act of surrender but a strategic withdrawal; their leader's parting words burned in Ryo's ears like a curse. He watched as the silhouettes of his attackers melted into the night, leaving behind only the echoes of their threats. Ryo sank to his knees, his breath ragged as he tried to steady himself.

Kota circled him, licking his hand in a gesture of comfort that belied the ferocity of their ordeal. The immediate danger had passed, but the confrontation had left a lingering dread in the pit of his stomach. The Rift Hunters would not be so easily deterred; their hunger for the power of the Timekeeper's Heart was insatiable, and they would return—stronger, more organized, and more ruthless than before.

In the silence that followed the battle, Ryo allowed himself a moment of reflection. The ground around him was scarred by the conflict— a mosaic of blood, dust, and broken metal that testified to the price of defiance in this fractured world. He clutched his spear tightly, the adrenaline slowly subsiding from his limbs, and then gazed at Kota. The dog's eyes shone with an inner light that Ryo now recognized as more than mere loyalty; they were the beacon of hope that held back the tide of chaos.

"Kota," Ryo whispered hoarsely,

"we have a long road ahead. They'll come back for you, for what you are… and we need to be ready." Kota's soft whine was the only answer he received. The bond between them—wrought from countless trials, silent understandings, and the fierce will to survive—was the one constant in a world stumbling on the edge of oblivion.

Slowly, Ryo rose and scanned the horizon. The rift behind them continued to pulse, its energies still turbulent but momentarily calmed by the sudden break in violence. Far in the distance, dark clouds gathered, and he could faintly detect the shapes of more of those hooded Hunters moving with renewed purpose. The battle had ended for now, but its aftershocks would ripple through time.

"We can't stop here," Ryo said, his voice low and determined.

"We have to keep moving. We have to find answers—about the shard, about Kota's power, and about how to stop them from using it to tear our world further apart."

With a final, lingering glance at the battered remnants of the battlefield, Ryo lifted Kota's leash. Together, they began the arduous trek away from the scene, their footprints imprinted in the dust as they retraced their steps toward the ruined city's labyrinthine streets. Each step felt weighted with the knowledge knowing that the Rift Hunter's plan was far from over.

Their enemy was not merely a band of ruthless scavengers, but a force intent on seizing control of time itself—a force that would stop at nothing to claim the power residing within Kota. Ryo's mind raced with plans and contingencies. He needed allies, knowledge, and a way to harness the very force that the Faction craved.

He resolved then that he would search for any sign of ancient myths—hidden libraries, underground vaults, or even the cryptic remnants of Kaori's words—that might help him understand the true nature of the Timekeeper's Heart. As the night deepened, the ruined city rose before them like a dark labyrinth of memories and shadows. The streets were eerily quiet, lit only by the intermittent glow of unstable rifts that punctuated the darkness like spectral beacons. Ryo's thoughts turned to the future, to the uncertain path that lay ahead—a path where every decision could either mend the fractured timeline or plunge it into further chaos.

In the distance, the sound of footsteps and muffled voices hinted at the presence of other survivors. Ryo's grip on his spear tightened as he quickened his pace, urging Kota to remain close. The battle had left him shaken but resolute. He knew that their enemy would not rest, and that each confrontation only brought him closer to the ultimate truth hidden within the tapestry of time. Navigating through narrow alleys and side streets, Ryo led Kota toward a small, partially intact building that had once served as a Museum. Its doors were ajar, and a faint light glimmered from within.

"Let's see if we can find some shelter—and perhaps some answers," Ryo murmured. He motioned for Kota to follow as he cautiously pushed open the door. Inside, the space was dim but surprisingly intact compared to the chaos outside. Dust motes danced in the beams of moonlight that streamed through broken windows, and remnants of old furniture and artifacts lay scattered about. It was a temporary refuge—a quiet haven amid the constant turmoil of the shattered city.

Ryo settled in a corner and took a moment to tend to his wounds with the care he could muster from salvaged supplies. Kota, ever alert, paced near the doorway, his ears twitching at every sound. As Ryo cleaned his cuts, his mind revisited the battle. The images of the Hunters, their leader's venomous words, and the surreal stabilization around Kota all played on a loop in his memory. He knew that the encounter was not an isolated incident—it was a calculated move by the Rift Hunters, a tactic to force him into a corner. In the silence of the temporary shelter, Ryo opened his journal and began to scribble notes frantically.

He recorded every detail of the ambush: the precise moment when the rift's energies had shifted, the way Kota's presence had momentarily tamed the chaotic swirl of light, and the chilling promises of the masked leader. Each word was a small act of defiance—a declaration that he would not let them control his destiny, nor the destiny of his beloved companion. As dawn approached, the first pale light filtered through the broken windows, and the remnants of the night's battle began to fade into a haze of memory.

Ryo rose, gathering his few belongings and checking that Kota was by his side. There was no time to rest—not when the dark forces that sought to exploit Kota's power were already regrouping in the shadows. With a final look at the battered walls of the Museum, Ryo stepped back into the uncertain light of morning. The city was stirring with the subdued activity of survivors, but behind every quiet street and every shadowed alley lay danger—and the constant reminder that the Rift Hunters' game plan was far from over. Determined, Ryo set his course for a distant district where he had heard whispers of an underground network of scholars and archivists.

They were said to guard fragments of old relics—secrets that might reveal the true nature of the Timekeeper's Heart and offer a way to thwart those who would use its power for destruction. Every step was fraught with uncertainty, but with Kota at his side—the living embodiment of hope and defiance—Ryo felt a flicker of optimism amidst the despair.

As they made their way through winding streets and past ruins bathed in the soft glow of a recovering sunrise, Ryo's thoughts remained fixed on the battle that had just been fought. The ambush had left scars not only on his body but on his soul. Their leader's promise, cold and merciless, echoed in his mind: that they would return, that they would capture Kota and wield his power to reshape time itself. This knowledge was a heavy burden, yet it also steeled his resolve. He would not allow that fate to befall them. The path ahead was uncertain and perilous. Every ruined building, every shadowed alley, held the potential for danger—and for discovery. Ryo clutched his spear tighter and kept a vigilant eye on the horizon.

With Kota's quiet, unyielding presence grounding him, he moved forward into the unknown. Every now and then, the memory of the convergence and the uncanny stabilization around Kota would flash in his mind, offering a momentary break from the harsh reality of their struggle. It was as though the universe had, for a fleeting instant, whispered that not all was lost—that in the bond between him and his faithful dog lay the seed of a future that could be reclaimed.

That thought, fragile as it was, propelled him onward. At the outskirts of the city, where the concrete gave way to the untamed wilds of the Wastes once more, Ryo paused to catch his breath. He surveyed the landscape: endless fields of cracked earth, the distant silhouettes of abandoned structures, and the soft hum of energy that seemed to emanate from the very ground beneath him. It was here, in the liminal space between civilization and oblivion, that Ryo resolved to prepare for what was to come.

He would seek out the underground network of archivists, gather any knowledge he could find, and fortify himself against the inevitable return of the Rift Hunters. Kota padded at his side, his eyes reflecting both caution and a quiet, unspoken understanding.

The battle was not yet over, and the stakes were higher than ever. As Ryo set off once again along the desolate road, his heart pounded with both dread and hope. The Hunters had made their plan—an audacious bid to seize the power of the Timekeeper's Heart—and Ryo knew that the coming days would be a test of trials, which one cannot prepare for. He vowed, as he walked into the uncertain future, that he would not let the darkness prevail.

For every threat that they posed, for every echo of their cruelty, he would answer with defiance and love—for Kota, for the fragments of time that still held promise, and for the future that might yet be salvaged from the ruins of the past. With the rising sun casting long shadows on the road ahead, Ryo and Kota pressed forward— two souls bound by fate, defying the forces that sought to enslave time itself.

The Rift Hunters' threat loomed large, but in the quiet determination of a man and his loyal companion lay a spark that could ignite a rebellion against the relentless march of darkness. And so, with each step echoing the beat of a resolute heart, Ryo walked into the dawn of a new day—a day that held the promise of answers, of battles yet to be fought, and of the enduring power of a bond that even time could not break.

Chapter 14: Crossing the Divide

The world around Ryo and Kota had become a vortex of fractured moments. After the brutal encounter with the Rift Hunters, their path had led them to a region where reality itself was unraveling—a place where the very air shimmered with unstable energy. They had heard whispers of a massive rift, a whirlpool of raw temporal power that had been growing in intensity for days, and now, as they moved along a desolate road, they could see its distorted glow pulsing in the distance like a beacon of both promise and peril.

Ryo squinted against the glare of that eerie light. The rift loomed ahead, an immense tear in the fabric of time, its edges writhing with turbulent hues of blue, violet, and sickly green. His heart pounded as he exchanged a determined glance with Kota, whose dark eyes were fixed on the shifting phenomenon. Every instinct told him that this was a place where the normal rules no longer applied—a place where the past, present, and future bled together into a single, unpredictable moment.

"We have to be careful," Ryo whispered, his voice steady despite the pounding in his chest.

"That rift... it's not just an anomaly; it's a trap waiting to swallow us whole." Kota growled softly in agreement, his ears perked and body low, as if bracing for the onslaught of energies that would soon overwhelm the senses. Ryo tightened his grip on his spear, a crude weapon forged from scavenged metal that had served him well in past battles. Every step toward the rift was a step deeper into the unknown.

They approached a narrow bend in the road where the unstable energies of the rift seemed to seep out into the world. The ground vibrated with a low, ominous hum that resonated through Ryo's boots and into his very bones. As he advanced, the air thickened and rippled, and moments later, the world around him began to distort. It started with subtle shifts—a flicker of light here, a sudden change in colour there—but soon, the landscape itself buckled under the pressure of conflicting timelines. In an instant, the familiar outlines of ruined buildings and desolate roads gave way to a surreal scene.

The horizon split into multiple overlapping images: one moment, Ryo saw the crumbling cityscape he'd known for so long; the next, he glimpsed a vision of a lush, vibrant world where sunlight bathed green parks and towering structures gleamed with life. The transitions were abrupt and disorienting, as if the rift were replaying snippets of what had been and what might be simultaneously.

"Kota, hold on!" Ryo shouted, his voice echoing strangely in the shifting air.

The dog barked, a sound filled with both fear and fierce determination, as if urging Ryo to fight against the oncoming chaos. Without warning, the ground beneath them buckled, and Ryo found himself off balance. The rift's energies surged violently, and a gust of wind ripped through the area, sending debris swirling around them in a frenzied dance. Ryo stumbled, barely managing to catch himself against a shattered wall. His heart raced as he struggled to steady both his mind and his footing.

Every sense was assaulted by the noise of overlapping voices, indistinct images, and the overwhelming pressure of time collapsing in on itself. Through the disorientation, Ryo could make out shapes moving, there were shadows that shifted too quickly to be real, fleeting figures that seemed to belong to eras long past. He pressed his hand to his temple, trying to anchor himself to the present.

"Stay with me, Kota," he urged, his voice trembling with determination.

"We have to get out of here." Kota, ever loyal, circled close and barked, as if to say that he was ready to fight alongside his master. Summoning every ounce of strength, Ryo scanned the area for any sign of an escape route. Amid the swirling chaos, he noticed a narrow passage between two collapsed structures—a corridor that, though unstable, might lead them away from the direct pull of the rift.

"Over there!" he pointed, and with Kota at his heels, he dashed toward the gap. The ground underfoot trembled with each step, and every so often, Ryo felt the crushing weight of conflicting timelines—a memory of the past intermingling with the urgency of the present.

The corridor was barely wide enough for him to squeeze through, with jagged remnants of debris hanging perilously overhead. Time here was erratic; seconds stretched into minutes, and the sound of his own heartbeat grew impossibly loud. As Ryo scrambled through the gap, the rift's chaotic energy lashed out, sending shards of light and debris crashing around him.

A beam of intense, shimmering light sliced across the passage, and for a moment, Ryo caught a glimpse of a future that was both wondrous and horrifying—a world rebuilt from the ashes, yet scarred by the eternal battle between order and chaos. The vision was over in an instant, leaving him gasping for breath and clinging to the wall for support. Kota, agile and fearless, led the way through the narrow exit. Once they emerged from the corridor, the landscape shifted again. They found themselves on the edge of a vast region—a desolate plain lit by a surreal, otherworldly glow.

The rift towered in the distance, its swirling vortex a constant reminder of the danger they had narrowly escaped. But here, away from the direct pull of the rift, the distortions had lessened to a disturbing calm. Ryo paused to catch his breath, leaning against a rock that jutted from the barren earth. His mind raced as he tried to make sense of the chaotic journey they had just endured.

Every second in the corridor had been a battle against the relentless tide of time itself. Now, as he looked back at the gap they had escaped from, he knew that the rift would not simply let them go. Its influence and its pull was far from over.

"Kota," Ryo said softly, kneeling to stroke the dog's fur as he regained his composure.

"We made it... for now. But they'll be coming for us again, and the rift... it's not done with us yet." Kota gazed up at him, eyes reflecting both fear and a quiet resolve, as if understanding every word without the need for translation.

The distant vortex continued to churn, and the horizon pulsed with the promise of both destruction and rebirth. Ryo knew that to truly escape the rift, he would need to find a way to sever its hold on their reality—to find a path that could mend the fractured threads of time rather than simply running from its chaos.

But for now, the immediate priority was to put as much distance as possible between themselves and the unstable epicentre. With cautious determination, Ryo hoisted his pack over his shoulder and signalled for Kota to move out. They retraced their steps along the edge of the plain, every footfall a measured act of defiance against the unyielding forces of the rift. The landscape here was more stable, though the lingering distortions served as a constant reminder that they were never truly free from the grasp of fractured time.

As they advanced, Ryo's thoughts turned to the warnings he had received—cryptic messages from Kaori, the strange signs in the Mirage Village, and the echoing voices of the past that still haunted his dreams.

Each of these had pointed to one undeniable truth: that Kota was not merely a dog but a living embodiment of hope—a beacon, the Timekeeper's Heart, capable of harmonizing the chaotic energies of a shattered timeline. In the cool, reflective light of dusk, as the plain stretched out before them like a barren canvas waiting to be rewritten, Ryo vowed to protect that hope.

"I won't let them take you, Kota," he whispered fiercely, his voice blending with the sighing wind.

"We'll find a way to mend what's broken. We'll forge a future where time is ours again." Kota's steady gaze and quiet bark served as both comfort and an unspoken pledge that he would stand by Ryo, no matter the odds. Together, they pressed onward along a narrow trail that snaked around the perimeter of the plain. The trail, marked by scattered pebbles and broken branches, wound through a series of gentle rises and falls.

With every step, the distant rift loomed larger, its chaotic energies a persistent backdrop to their flight. At one particularly steep section of the trail, the ground trembled violently. Ryo stumbled, nearly losing his balance as the vibrations grew stronger. For a terrifying moment, the air around him shimmered and the world blurred into a swirl of disjointed images. He could see fragments of the past—a child's laughter, a burst of sunlight through an ancient tree—and flashes of what might be: a city rebuilt, a future where hope prevailed.

The vision was fleeting, and as quickly as it came, it was replaced by the relentless present. Ryo pressed on, heart pounding, as the ground finally steadied beneath him. He looked at Kota, whose eyes shone with an inner light that seemed to challenge the darkness.

"We're almost there, boy," Ryo said softly,

though he wasn't sure what "there" meant—only that every step away from the rift was a step toward reclaiming some order. The trail opened onto a small cliff, offering a brief pause from the chaotic energy that had dominated their journey.

Here, the landscape was dotted with ancient boulders and patches of resilient wildflowers that defied the barren earth. The distant hum of the rift was still audible, a constant reminder that the fractured threads of time were never far away. Ryo sank onto a large, smooth stone and pulled Kota close, taking a moment to catch his breath. The quiet of the plateau was deceptive—a fragile calm in the midst of a world that could shatter at any moment. He gazed out over the vast plain, his eyes lingering on the distant vortex that pulsed with a hypnotic, almost malignant energy.

"Escape isn't as simple as running away," Ryo murmured, more to himself than to Kota.

"It's about finding a way to live with the chaos—to bend it to our will, if only for a moment." He closed his eyes and listened to the wind, which carried the faint, discordant melody of the rift. In that sound, he thought he could hear a promise—a whisper that, somewhere in the depths of chaos, lay the seed of renewal. For several long minutes, Ryo sat in reflective silence. He thought of the battles fought, and the truth that had been revealed: that the power within

Kota was a double-edged sword—a gift that could restore balance or plunge the world into further ruin if misused. The Hunters would not rest until they harnessed that power, and Ryo knew that his fight was far from over. Determined to gain an advantage, Ryo stood and dusted himself off.

"We need to find shelter for the night," he said, his voice firm.

"Rest, regroup, and plan our next move." Kota barked in agreement, his tail wagging in a brief show of optimism. They began their descent from the plateau, carefully retracing their steps along the narrow, winding trail. Every sound, every shifting shadow, was a potential threat. The rift's distant glow pulsed on the horizon—a stark reminder that its chaotic influence was ever-present.

Yet, even in the face of such overwhelming force, Ryo's resolve burned bright. The bond he shared with Kota was their most precious asset, and as long as that bond endured, there was hope. After several hours of cautious travel, they arrived at a crumbling stone structure that had once served as a small outpost. Its walls, though scarred by time and neglect, still provided a degree of protection from the elements and prying eyes. Ryo secured the door as best he could, then settled inside with Kota at his side.

The interior was dim and musty, but it offered a temporary haven from the relentless uncertainty of the wasteland. By the light of a salvaged lantern, Ryo spread out a tattered map and a few scraps of old notes he had gathered along his journey. He pored over them, trying to distinguish a pattern—a route that might lead away from the rift's influence and toward a place of stability.

The map was incomplete, pieced together from scattered fragments of memory and rumour, but it hinted at the existence of a safe zone deep within the remnants of the old city—a place where the chaotic energies might be less pronounced. Kota lay near Ryo's feet, his presence a steady comfort as the night deepened. Outside, the distant rumble of the rift was a constant reminder that danger lurked beyond the thin walls of their refuge.

Ryo's eyes were heavy with exhaustion, but sleep would have to wait. There was too much at stake, and every moment of rest was a moment closer to the next onslaught. Ryo scribbled down plans and possibilities, his mind racing with strategies to outmaneuver the relentless forces that pursued them.

The threat loomed large, and he knew that escaping the rift was only the beginning of a long, perilous journey.

The fractured timeline was like a living labyrinth, and every decision he made would echo through the days to come. As midnight approached, the air outside turned bitterly cold. Ryo wrapped himself in a threadbare blanket and tried to catch a few moments of rest, though his mind remained alert to every creak of the building and every gust of wind that might signal danger. Kota's soft, rhythmic breathing was the only sound that offered reassurance in the oppressive silence. In the half-light of the early hours, Ryo awoke with a start to the sound of distant shouts—a reminder that the Rift Hunters were not far behind.

He hurriedly gathered his belongings and peered out the broken window. Far off in the darkness, silhouettes moved against the horizon—hunters on the prowl, drawn by the scent of power and defiance. Ryo's heart pounded, but he knew that retreat was not an option. The rift, with all its destructive potential, was a force that would shape their destiny whether they fought it or fled from it.

"Kota," Ryo whispered urgently,

"we have to move—now." The dog lifted his head, eyes alert, and let out a soft, determined bark. Together, they slipped out of the shelter into the frigid night. The path ahead was cloaked in uncertainty, but Ryo's resolve was unwavering.

Every step would be a gamble against fate, but the promise of a future free from the Hunters' grasp and the rift's relentless pull spurred him on.

The cold night air stung Ryo's face as he led Kota along narrow alleys and through darkened streets. The distant hum of the rift provided a constant, pulsating backdrop—a reminder that even as they sought to escape, the chaotic energies of fractured time were never far away.

Ryo's thoughts were heavy with the burden of responsibility: to protect Kota, the living embodiment of hope, and to forge a path toward a tomorrow where the wounds of the past might finally begin to heal. As they moved deeper into the labyrinth of the ruined city, the familiar landmarks faded into obscurity, replaced by crumbling walls and deserted passages. Every shadow could hide an enemy, every sound could be the signal of another ambush.

Ryo clutched his spear tightly, every sense on high alert as he navigated the maze-like passages of the city's underbelly. At one point, as they rounded a corner, a sudden burst of light exploded in the distance—a rift flaring up unexpectedly, its chaotic energy washing over the street in violent waves.

The ground trembled beneath their feet, and Ryo's heart raced as he dove behind a collapsed wall. Kota, ever brave, remained by his side, his eyes fixed on the thunderous spectacle. For several excruciating moments, the rift's fury dominated the night, sending a shockwave of distorted time through the city. Ryo huddled in the darkness, praying that the Rift Hunters would not use this moment to close in on them. When the light finally subsided and the trembling ceased, the street lay silent once more—but the memory of that violent surge lingered, a stark reminder of the rift's unpredictable nature. Ryo rose cautiously, helping Kota to his feet.

"We can't let our guard down," he said in a low voice.

"Not for a second. They'll be back, and so will that rift's pull." Determination set in his eyes as he resumed his journey. Every step was a calculated risk, every turn a potential ambush.

Yet, driven by the fierce desire to escape the relentless grasp of chaos and to forge a new future for himself and his loyal companion, Ryo pressed on. The city slowly began to give way to a more open region—a liminal zone between the dense urban ruins and the wild, untamed Wastes beyond.

Here, the buildings were fewer and farther between, and the night sky stretched out in all its starry luxury. The rift's glow was a distant, pulsing presence on the horizon, less menacing but ever-constant. Ryo paused at the crest of a small hill, taking in the panoramic view of the ruined city below. The landscape was a patchwork of shadow and light—a chaotic quilt of desolation and hope. In the distance, the silhouettes of survivors moved like ghosts among the wreckage, their lives a fragile defiance against the ravages of time. It was in this moment of relative calm that Ryo allowed himself a brief moment of reflection.

The battle with the Hunters, the chaos of the rift, and the crushing weight of his responsibility all converged within him. Yet, amid the darkness, the bond with Kota shone like a guiding star, a reminder that hope was not lost. He knelt down, stroking Kota's fur gently, and whispered,

"We're not done fighting, boy. Not yet. But as long as we're together, there's a future worth claiming."

Kota responded with a soft, affirming bark, and Ryo's eyes filled with resolve. Determined to find a safer route and to regroup for the battles ahead, Ryo studied the map he had pieced together from scattered clues and survivor whispers. There was talk of a secure enclave—a refuge deep within the ruins of an old governmental district—where a community of scholars and warriors had banded together to resist the dark forces of the fractured world. It was there, he hoped, that he might find the knowledge and resources necessary to counter the Rift Hunters and to eventually mend the fractured timeline.

As they moved along the deserted road, the sounds of the city gave way to the soft murmur of the natural world—the rustle of leaves, the distant call of nocturnal creatures, and the gentle lapping of a nearby stream.

The environment, though scarred by the passage of time and the remnants of human endeavour, offered a fragile sense of peace. In this delicate stillness, Ryo found a moment of clarity—a vision of what could be if the shattered fragments of time were not left to drift aimlessly. But even as hope stirred within him, the ever-present threat of the Rift Hunters loomed. The night deepened as Ryo and Kota pressed on. Every now and then, a sudden rustle or a fleeting shadow set Ryo's nerves on edge, but he continued with determined resolve.

The path was uncertain and treacherous, yet the bond with Kota gave him strength—a reminder that even in the fractured tapestry of time, the human spirit could still find a way to persevere. Finally, as the first hints of dawn began to tint the horizon with pale blue light, Ryo reached a crossroads—a narrow, cobbled street flanked by crumbling stone walls that led toward an area known to be less frequented by hostile forces. He paused, catching his breath, and consulted his makeshift map.

This was the point where he would veer away from the central ruins and head toward the rumoured enclave of scholars.

"Kota, we're almost there," Ryo said softly, his voice filled with cautious optimism. The loyal dog responded with a gentle bark, as if sensing that their trials were nearing a turning point. Together, they stepped onto the cobbled street, leaving behind the chaotic echoes of the rift and the harried night of escape.

Ryo's journey was far from over; the path ahead would demand sacrifices and tests of resolve, but with Kota by his side, he was determined to face whatever challenges awaited. As the sun's first rays began to illuminate the broken skyline, Ryo took one last look over his shoulder at the dark region from which he had escaped—a realm of ever-shifting time and dangerous power. Then, with a steady gaze and a heart full of resolve, he pressed onward into the uncertain dawn.

Chapter 15: Mirrored Streets

Ryo squinted against the glare of an early autumn sun as he and Kota emerged from a narrow, debris-strewn passageway leading away from the chaotic urban ruins. Before them lay a sight that seemed almost surreal—a city that defied the ravages of the Time Rapture by appearing suspended in an unyielding moment. The city's skyline, once vibrant with modern promise, now rose in ghostly silhouettes, its buildings preserved as if trapped in a perfect instant. The air here was different—calmer, almost reverent—as though the world itself had paused to remember. The gentle murmur of wind and distant, measured drips of water echoed through immaculate streets where not a trace of decay marred the architecture.

Pavements, sidewalks, and windows gleamed under a light that was both soft and otherworldly. Ryo's heart pounded with a mixture of awe and wariness. How could such a place exist amid the fractured timeline? Had this city truly been spared from chaos, or was it itself a trap—a remnant of an experiment to freeze time? Kota padded at his side, his ears perked and eyes alert, as if sensing the peculiar stillness that enveloped the city. Ryo recalled the hushed legends he'd heard among survivors: whispers of a "Timeless City" that existed in a pocket of the shattered world, where time itself had been suspended to preserve lost knowledge.

With each step toward the looming entrance of a grand, ancient archway at the city's heart, Ryo felt the weight of possibility and mystery grow heavier. They entered the city through a wide boulevard framed by towering columns and decorated elevations. The buildings, though grand, bore no signs of human activity. Instead, their interiors were frozen in mid-life—a café with chairs set in a perfect arrangement, an open market stall with goods still arranged as if awaiting customers, even a park where a swing swayed imperceptibly in the still air. It was as if every moment in this city had been captured at the peak of life, a single frame of what once was.

Yet an eerie silence reigned—a silence that was both mournful and strangely hopeful. Ryo led Kota along the boulevard, his footsteps echoing against smooth marble and polished stone. He couldn't shake the feeling that every surface, every carving on the walls, held a message—a message that could reveal secrets of the past and perhaps a way to mend what had been broken. As they walked, Ryo's eyes lingered on murals and inscriptions adorning the exteriors of buildings. They depicted scenes of vibrant life: children playing in sunlit gardens, families gathered around long tables, elders sharing wisdom beneath starlit skies.

It was a tapestry of memory, preserved with immaculate care. At the centre of the city, Ryo discovered a vast public square. In the middle stood an enormous clock tower, its clock face encircled by elaborate carvings and symbols that he did not recognize. Strangely, the clock's hands were frozen at exactly 10:10—a detail that sent a shiver down his spine. It was as if the moment of the city's preservation was marked in time, forever encapsulated in that singular instance.

Ryo approached the tower slowly, Kota at his heel. He reached out and touched the cool stone of the clock's base, feeling a gentle vibration beneath his fingertips—almost like the beating of a giant, ancient heart. He wondered if this was the key: if understanding the mechanism behind this frozen moment could reveal the means to restore the flow of time, or at least, to mend the fractured spectrum that had left so many worlds in ruins. A sudden sound drew Ryo's attention—a faint footstep echoing across the square.

He turned sharply, hand going to his worn knife, only to see a figure emerge from the shadows. A young woman stepped forward; her eyes were bright and filled with a quiet urgency. She wore a simple dress, and a delicate silver pendant hung around her neck—a small, intricately designed gear that shimmered in the soft light.

"Welcome," she said, her voice gentle but carrying a note of determination.

"I have been waiting for you." Ryo's guard remained raised.

"Who are you?" he asked cautiously, his voice low.

"My name is Liana," the woman replied, stepping closer with measured grace.

"I am a keeper of the city's memory. I know the secrets of this place—secrets that have been hidden for generations." Her eyes flickered to Kota, and for a moment, Ryo thought he saw recognition in them.

"Your companion," she continued,

"is not an ordinary creature. He carries the essence of time within him, a spark of the power that once healed the broken strands of our world." Liana continues.

"In our legends, he is known as the Timekeeper's Heart—a living beacon of hope that keeps the past and future intertwined. His presence here is no accident. This city, preserved in time, exists because it was built on the foundation of forgotten knowledge, and your companion embodies that knowledge."

As Liana spoke, the square around them seemed to come alive with whispers—echoes of voices from a time when the city had thrived. Ryo felt as if the air itself vibrated with the memories of countless souls, each one a piece of a vast mosaic that had been carefully preserved. The grandeur of the Timeless City, with its immaculate structures and quiet dignity, was both a refuge and a repository of wisdom lost to the ravages of the Time Rapture.

"Why is this city frozen in time?" Ryo asked, his voice hushed as if speaking to a sacred secret. Liana smiled sadly.

"Long ago, when the Time Rapture shattered the world, the elders of this city made a desperate choice. They activated an ancient mechanism—a pact with forces beyond our understanding—to preserve the knowledge of our people. In doing so, they trapped the city in a single moment—a moment of perfection, of hope, and of mourning. We exist here as living echoes, relics of what once was. But we also guard a secret: that if the scattered pieces of time can be gathered, there is a way to mend the fractures." Liana's gaze softened as she regarded the loyal dog.

"I have seen visions. In the stillness of this city, the bond between you and your dog shines like a beacon. It is said that when the Timekeeper's Heart is reunited with the lost fragments of our knowledge, the cycle of despair can be broken. I believe you both are part of that destiny." Ryo's mind raced with questions and possibilities.

Here, in this Timeless City, lay the remnants of a past that had been so meticulously preserved—and perhaps, the tools to forge a future once more.

"Then teach me," he said finally, his voice steady with resolve.

"Teach me the secrets of this city, and tell me how we can use what lies here to restore time."

Liana extended a hand, inviting him to follow her through the labyrinthine corridors of the city.

"Come with me," she said softly.

"There is much to learn, and every moment here is a gift. Within these walls, the elders recorded their wisdom in symbols, murals, and texts. The key to mending our world lies not in destroying the past, but in understanding it and using its lessons to shape the future."

They walked together along wide boulevards and down narrow alleys lined with crumbling stone and decorative archways. Liana pointed out faded inscriptions on walls, relics of a time when the city was a centre of learning and innovation. In one grand hall, an enormous mural depicted a tree with branches reaching out to the heavens, its roots intertwined with countless clocks and gears—a vivid representation of time's interconnected nature. In another corner, ancient manuscripts lay preserved in glass cases, their fragile pages containing diagrams of temporal energy and charts that promised renewal.

Ryo listened intently as Liana explained the history of the city.

"Our ancestors believed that time was like a river—a force that could be dammed or channeled. When the Time Rapture came, they sought to preserve the best of what was, to hold onto hope even as the world fell apart. They built this city as a sanctuary of knowledge, a place where the past would never be forgotten. And now, it is your destiny to take that knowledge and use it to guide us forward."

As they crossed the city, the air seemed to hum with quiet energy—a soft, persistent vibration that resonated with Ryo's very soul. He could feel it in the gentle brush of wind, in the subtle gleam of sunlight on polished stone, and in the steady gaze of Kota, who walked as if he were the guardian of every secret hidden within these walls.

They arrived at the central library, an imposing structure with tall, arched windows and columns decorated with intricate carvings. Inside, dust motes danced in beams of sunlight that filtered through the broken glass, and rows upon rows of books and scrolls filled the vast hall. This was the heart of the city's wisdom, the repository of generations of knowledge that had been preserved against the ravages of time.

Liana led Ryo to a secluded nook deep within the library.

"Here," she said,

"you will find the Chronicle of Ages." She gently pulled a large, leather-bound volume from a weathered shelf. The cover was embossed with symbols that glowed faintly, as if injected with their own timeless light.

Ryo opened the book carefully, his fingers tracing the delicate script and elaborate diagrams that detailed the history of the city, the secrets of temporal energy, and the prophecy of the Timekeeper's Heart. With each page he turned, he felt as though he were peeling back the layers of a vast, intricate tapestry—a tapestry that wove together the past, present, and future in a single, eternal moment.

"This chronicle," Liana explained,

"contains the wisdom of our ancestors. It speaks of the time when the world was whole, of the beauty that once existed, and of the sacrifice required to preserve that beauty. It also foretells a day when the Timekeeper's Heart—embodied by a living guardian—would be the catalyst for mending the broken strands of time."

Ryo's eyes widened as he read passages that described a creature of pure, unyielding spirit— one whose heartbeat resonated with the pulse of the universe.

The words resonated deeply with him, for they described not only the history of the Timeless City but also the destiny that now lay before him.

"I… I never imagined," he whispered, closing the book gently.

"I always thought I was just surviving, but now… it seems I have a purpose." Liana nodded, her expression a mixture of relief and sadness.

"It is both a gift and a burden. To carry the hope of the past and the promise of the future on your shoulders is no easy task. But the knowledge contained within this chronicle is not meant to be hoarded—it is meant to be shared, to guide us as we strive to restore what was lost." Outside the library, the Timeless City continued to exist in a state of suspended grace—a city caught between memory and possibility. The streets, the statues, and the faded murals all bore testament to a people who had once believed in the power of knowledge and the beauty of time.

Ryo felt the weight of that legacy, and with each breath, he vowed to honour it. As the day wore on, Ryo and Kota, guided by Liana's insights, wandered through the city. They studied the murals in the public square, the inscriptions carved into stone, and the remnants of technological marvels that hinted at a civilization far advanced before the collapse. Every detail was a clue—a fragment of a larger puzzle that, when assembled, might reveal the key to restoring time. In one particularly vivid corner of the city, Ryo discovered a quiet garden nestled between two grand structures.

The garden was a riot of colours—flowers of every hue blossomed amid carefully tended hedges and bubbling fountains that still worked, powered by a mysterious, undying energy. It was here, in this oasis of life amid the stillness of the Timeless City, that Ryo felt a moment of profound connection.

He sat on a stone bench, Kota curled up at his feet, and allowed himself to be enveloped by the fragrance of blooming jasmine and the gentle murmur of water.

"This is what we lost," Ryo murmured, his eyes glistening.

"The beauty, the joy… the very essence of life. And perhaps, it is also what we can reclaim." The garden, a preserved memory of the world as it once was, kindled within him a spark of determination.

If he could learn from these remnants and unlock the secrets of the past, maybe there was a way to mend the broken world.

As dusk approached, Liana rejoined them in the garden.

"You have seen the legacy of our people," she said softly.

"But remember, the chronicle also speaks of a final trial—a test that will determine whether the bonds of time can be restored. That trial lies beyond these walls, in the heart of the Timeless City, where the energies of the past and future converge. Only by facing that trial can you hope to harness the power of the Timekeeper's Heart and use it to heal our world." Ryo looked from Liana to Kota, feeling the enormity of his burden—and the depth of his resolve.

"Then I will face it," he declared, voice firm.

"I won't let the legacy of this city, or the hope embodied in Kota, fade into oblivion. I will learn, I will fight, and I will strive to build a future that honours the past." Liana's eyes shone with quiet admiration.

"Go forth. The Timeless City has given you its wisdom. Now, it is up to you to carry that wisdom into the darkness and ignite a light that can guide us all toward renewal." With that, she stepped away into the fading light, leaving Ryo alone in the garden with Kota and the echoes of ancient promises.

The sky overhead was a tapestry of deep blues and soft purples as night fell, and the first stars began to twinkle in the heavens. The garden, bathed in moonlight, seemed to pulse with a serene vibrancy—a stark contrast to the desolation that lay beyond the city's borders.

Ryo gathered his belongings and, with Kota trotting faithfully by his side, set out toward the next phase of his journey. His destination was a hidden enclave rumoured to house the last of the archivists—a community of scholars and survivors dedicated to preserving the true history of the Time Rapture.

If there was a way to harness the power of the Timekeeper's Heart, Ryo believed it lay within the combined knowledge of these keepers of memory. As he walked through the winding, lantern-lit streets of the Timeless City, Ryo felt the pulse of history beneath his feet. Every step was a connection to those who had come before him—the dreamers, the fighters, the lovers and the lost. He vowed silently that he would not let their sacrifices be in vain.

With each conversation he held, each mural he studied, he pieced together the mosaic of his world's former glory, and in doing so, he forged the path to its possible rebirth. Hours later, in a narrow back alley lined with crumbling stone and flickering lanterns, Ryo finally reached a modest building marked by a faded insignia—a symbol he recognized from the chronicle as representing the ancient archivists. Taking a deep breath, he stepped inside. The interior was cramped but filled with shelves of fragile books, scrolls, and relics.

The air was thick with the scent of parchment and ink—a library of memory preserved against all odds. An elderly archivist, his face lined with the wisdom of many years, looked up from a desk cluttered with notes and maps. "You have come," the archivist said in a quiet, measured tone.

"I knew you would come." Ryo bowed his head respectfully.

"I am Ryo, and this is Kota. I seek knowledge, any clue that can help us restore the flow of time and save our future." The archivist's eyes, deep and sorrowful, softened as he motioned for Ryo to sit.

"The Timeless City holds many secrets, young one. Within these pages lie the memories of a world that once was—a world of beauty, wisdom, and unity. But more than that, they hold the key to mending the fractures that now threaten us all." He reached for an ancient manuscript bound in cracked leather.

"Here is the 'Codex of Renewal,' a record of the prophecy that foretold the rise of the Timekeeper's Heart. It speaks of a day when one bond—between a man and his faithful companion—would become the spark to ignite a new beginning." Ryo's hands trembled as he took the codex and carefully opened it. The manuscript was filled with elaborate diagrams of gears, celestial bodies, and intricate symbols that intertwined with lyrical verses describing a destiny that spanned beyond time.

As he read, Ryo felt tears prick his eyes—tears born of hope, loss, and the overwhelming burden of responsibility. The words were both a comfort and a challenge: a promise that if he could unlock the mysteries of the past, there might be a way to rebuild the future. Over the next several hours, Ryo studied over the codex alongside the archivist, absorbing every nuance of the prophecy. The archivist explained that the Timekeeper's Heart was not merely a title bestowed upon Kota—it was a living testament to the possibility that the fractures in time could be healed if the right balance were restored.

"The bond you share with Kota," the archivist said softly,

"is the bridge between what has been lost and what might be regained. It is the foundation upon which a new era can be built." As night deepened outside, Ryo left the sanctuary of the archivists' haven with the codex securely in his pack. The Timeless City had shown him the beauty of what once was and the potential for what could be again. Stepping back out into the cool night air, Ryo paused at the edge of a quiet square where the ancient clock still stood—a silent guardian of a moment long frozen.

The clock tower's hands remained at 10:10, a poignant reminder of the day the city was preserved in time.

Kota, sensing the gravity of the moment, rested his head on Ryo's knee. In that simple, steadfast gesture, Ryo felt the strength of their bond—a bond that would carry him through the darkest of nights and the most turbulent of temporal storms. With determination etched into every line of his face, Ryo resumed his journey through the Timeless City, the city around him, though frozen in a singular moment, continued to whisper its ancient secrets. And as Ryo walked onward, the words of the codex echoed in his mind: that the power to restore time lay not in forcing it to conform, but in embracing the natural flow of memory, love, and hope.

Yet, armed with knowledge, determination, and the unbreakable bond with his faithful companion, he vowed to keep fighting—until the broken strands of time could finally be woven together into a tapestry of new beginnings.

Chapter 16: Voices Between

The air was electric with the soft hum of ancient energies as Ryo and Kota trudged along a forgotten road that cut between the fractured remnants of the old city and the wild, untamed lands beyond. It was early morning—the light, though pale and diffused, carried an unusual clarity that hinted at the hidden wonders lying in wait. Ryo's thoughts were heavy with the lessons of the past few days, with every step laden by the promise of mystery and the burden of destiny.

But today, something felt different. Today, the very earth seemed to pulse with a rhythm that resonated deep within his bones—a rhythm that matched the steady beat of Kota's heart. Ryo paused at the crest of a low hill and looked out over the barren area below. Far off, on the horizon, a shimmering band of light causing a ripple in the sky. It was not a rift as he had seen before, nor was it the ghostly echo of a fractured memory. This was something new—a visible manifestation of temporal energy that seemed to beckon him forward. He could almost hear the soft cadence of a cosmic heartbeat, faint but insistent, calling him to step into the unknown.

"Kota, do you feel that?" Ryo murmured, kneeling down on the cool, cracked earth. The Shiba Inu sat quietly beside him, his dark eyes fixed on the distant glow as if understanding every word. For the first time in weeks, Ryo felt that the mysterious power within Kota—the essence that made him the Timekeeper's Heart—was about to reveal itself in full force. Slowly, Ryo rose and began to descend the hill. Every step felt charged with possibility. As he walked, the wind carried subtle whispers—fragmented voices that spoke of forgotten days, of lost love and unfulfilled dreams. The sound was haunting yet comforting, as if the past itself was reaching out to him with gentle encouragement.

Ryo clutched his makeshift spear tighter, not out of fear, but in anticipation of what was to come. After several minutes, the road led them into a valley encircled by ancient, moss-covered stone walls that rose from the earth like the ruins of a long-lost fortress. Here, the air was cooler and more saturated with energy.

Ryo could see faint patterns in the ground—delicate, almost imperceptible lines that pulsed with a rhythmic glow, like the traces of an old circuit long forgotten by time. The path ahead seemed to narrow, guiding them toward the centre of this natural amphitheater where the light on the horizon grew ever brighter. As they approached, Ryo's eyes widened in awe. In the centre of the valley lay a circular clearing. At its heart was a large, weathered obelisk covered in ancient symbols and intricate carvings. The stone structure exuded a soft luminescence that merged seamlessly with the strange, undulating light above. The obelisk appeared to vibrate with an inner energy—a silent drumbeat that seemed to synchronize with the rhythm of the valley itself. Ryo stepped forward, his heart pounding in unison with the pulsing energy. Kota trotted beside him, occasionally pausing to sniff at the air as if drawn by an invisible force. When they reached the obelisk, Ryo placed a trembling hand on its cool surface. In that moment, the valley seemed to hold its breath.

The ancient stone responded, and a gentle pulse radiated outward, rippling across the clearing in concentric circles. A deep, resonant hum filled the space, building steadily until it felt as though the very ground was alive with sound.

Ryo closed his eyes, and the visions began. He saw flashes of moments that spanned centuries—glimpses of the past intermingled with hints of futures yet to be written. There were scenes of bustling marketplaces from a world that once was, serene images of lovers parting under a starlit sky, and echoes of battles fought long ago. Amid these shifting images, one constant shone clearly: the image of Kota, his faithful companion, appearing in countless forms—a playful pup in one vision, a steadfast guardian in another, his eyes alight with an inner brilliance that defied the ravages of time.

When Ryo opened his eyes, the world around him had transformed. The once-muted hues of the valley were now vibrant with colour, and the obelisk glowed with an intensity that seemed to merge the past, present, and future into one luminous tapestry. The light on the horizon had descended, enveloping the clearing in a celestial glow. The energy was overwhelming, yet it felt as if it was speaking directly to him—a silent affirmation that the power of the Timekeeper's Heart was real, and that it could be a force for renewal.

"Kota…" Ryo whispered, kneeling down and drawing the loyal dog close. In that moment, the bond between them felt visible, almost as though it could bridge the gap between broken time and uncharted possibility. The gentle vibration of the obelisk, the hum of the earth, and the soft murmur of ancient voices all converged to create an overwhelming sense of resonance—a confirmation that their journey was intertwined with the very fabric of time.

Ryo slowly pulled out the blue shard from his pack—a fragment he had recovered in the ruins, whose glow had always seemed to mirror Kota's presence. He held it up to the light, and the shard began to pulse in synchrony with the ancient stone. The sight filled him with both wonder and a profound sense of responsibility.

The shard was more than a remnant of the past; it was a key—a tangible piece of the mystery that might unlock the secrets of the Time Rapture. As the light of the obelisk grew brighter, Ryo felt a surge of energy course through him. The vision intensified, and he saw a montage of images: the creation of the obelisk in ancient times, the forging of a bond between man and creature during moments of great peril, and the coming together of scattered fragments of a shattered timeline. In every scene, Kota was there, his presence a constant, reassuring beacon amid the chaos of time.

The realization struck Ryo like a jolt of lightning: the very bond he shared with his companion was a source of power—a power that could perhaps mend what had been broken. Tears welled in Ryo's eyes as he whispered,

"You are the heart of time, Kota. You carry within you the hope of tomorrow." Kota's eyes shone back at him, filled with an unspoken understanding that transcended words. In that charged moment, the valley, the obelisk, and the shard all converged into a single, transcendent reality—a resonance that bound the past to the future, and infused the present with an almost sacred promise. The hum of the obelisk began to recede slowly, and the visions faded as the clearing returned to its serene state.

The celestial glow softened, leaving behind a gentle radiance that seemed to linger in the air. Ryo exhaled slowly, his heart still racing with the enormity of what he had witnessed. He gently caressed Kota's fur, silently vowing to protect the secret of his extraordinary companion. For several long minutes, Ryo stood there in quiet contemplation. He understood now that the Timekeeper's Resonance was not just a fleeting phenomenon, but an invitation to take action—a sign that the fractured strands of time could be realigned if only one had the courage to nurture the bonds that held them together.

The obelisk had spoken: the power to restore balance lay not in wielding force against the chaos, but in embracing the quiet strength of connection, memory, and hope. Slowly, Ryo gathered the shard and tucked it safely back into his pack. With Kota by his side, he turned away from the obelisk and began to retrace his steps along the narrow path that led out of the valley. The shimmering light of the convergence still danced in his mind, a reminder of what was possible if he could harness the Timekeeper's Resonance. He knew the journey ahead would be fraught with challenges—foes would seek to exploit this newfound power, and the dark forces that had fractured time would not easily relinquish their hold.

Yet, in that quiet, powerful moment, Ryo felt a surge of hope that was impossible to ignore. As they left the valley behind, the landscape gradually resumed its familiar, rugged appearance. The once-unstable energies of the rift in the distance still pulsed on the horizon, but here on the narrow path, the world had a temporary, fragile order. Ryo walked with a new sense of purpose—each step filled with the determination to protect Kota, to nurture the power within him, and to seek out the hidden allies and ancient knowledge that might one day mend the shattered timeline. In the days that followed, Ryo found himself haunted by the memory of the resonance.

Every time he caught a glimpse of Kota's steady, unwavering gaze or felt the soft pulse of the blue shard against his chest, he was reminded of that sacred moment in the valley. The vision of the obelisk and the chorus of ancient voices lingered in his dreams, urging him to press forward into the unknown. At night, as Ryo lay awake in his makeshift shelter among the ruins, he would often trace the patterns on the blue shard with his fingertip, feeling the faint vibrations that echoed the rhythm of the Timekeeper's Heart. He began to document his experiences in his battered journal—recording not only the physical journey but the profound emotional and spiritual awakening that had been ignited by the resonance. Each entry was a testament to the fragile hope that had emerged from the chaos—a hope that even in a world shattered by the collapse of time, the bonds of memory and love could pave the way to renewal.

As Ryo and Kota continued their journey, the landscape shifted subtly with the passage of days. The chaos of the fractured city slowly gave way to more stable, if still desolate, terrain. Yet, every so often, Ryo would catch a fleeting glimpse of the valley—a reminder of the profound moment when time itself had spoken to him. Those memories fuelled his determination as he navigated the treacherous roads, facing hostile scavengers, treacherous rifts, and the ever-looming threat of the Rift Hunters who sought to exploit Kota's unique gift. Despite the dangers, Ryo found moments of quiet beauty along the way. In a long-forgotten garden reclaimed by nature, he would pause to admire the resilient bloom of a single flower pushing through cracked concrete—a symbol, he thought, of the possibility of rebirth.

In the soft murmur of a quiet stream, he heard the echoes of ancient songs, as if the water itself remembered the lullabies of a world before the Rapture. And always, by his side, was Kota—steady, brave, and luminous with the quiet power that Ryo now understood was the very heartbeat of time. One crisp morning, as the sun rose with an uncharacteristic brilliance, Ryo found himself at the edge of a small plateau overlooking a vast region of restored light. The Timekeeper's Resonance had shown him that the power to restore balance was not lost; it lived in the quiet strength of connection and in the steadfast heart of his loyal companion.

"Tomorrow, we move toward the archives," Ryo said softly to Kota, his voice filled with a mixture of resolve and anticipation.

"There is knowledge out there that can guide us—and together, we will unlock it." Kota responded with a gentle bark, his eyes reflecting the unspoken promise of a future forged from the bonds of the past. And so, with the echoes of the valley still resounding in his heart, Ryo and Kota journeyed on. Every step was an act of defiance against the chaos that had shattered time, every heartbeat a promise that hope would persist.

Chapter 17: Forgotten Records

The first light of dawn broke over the shattered city in cold, pale shafts that glinted off ruined spires and the slick ribbon of the canal below. Ryo paused atop a fractured overpass, spear in hand, and took in the scene: jagged steel beams where trains once ran, collapsed towers leaning into the morning mist, and the low, persistent hum of chronological energy that seemed to pulse from deep beneath the streets.

At his side, Kota sat alert, ears swivelled forward as though reading the city's broken heartbeat. In two days they'd tracked the hum to this district—once the cultural heart of the metropolis, now a graveyard of time's ambitions.

Ryo slid the sensor from his pack; its needle spun wild before settling into a steady buzz, pointing down a narrow alley choked with rubble.

"Here," he said softly. Kota sniffed at the debris and, with a small bark, began nosing through the concrete fragments until a rectangular steel hatch came into view, half-buried and rusted. The sensor glowed brighter against its surface. Ryo crouched and pried at the edges, freeing the hatch to reveal a ladder descending into darkness. Ryo glanced at Kota. The dog's fur bristled with excitement.

"All right, boy—let's see what they left behind."

The ladder's steps were slick with moss, and each creaked under Ryo's weight. Kota padded down behind him, paws echoing on metal. At the bottom lay a narrow tunnel, its walls lined with ancient glyphs half-erased by water and time. Faint blue veins of light pulsed along the stone—residual wards still faintly holding back the tide of fractured time. Ryo activated his lamp, the beam slicing through the gloom.

"These wards—old Time Weavers," he murmured, tracing the symbols.

"They built this place to protect knowledge, to guard the flow of time itself." Kota pressed forward, the corridor widening into a series of arched halls. Dust motes drifted in the lamplight. Ryo's footsteps echoed, but beneath them he felt something else—a subtle vibration, like the whisper of a distant heartbeat.

They emerged into a vast chamber. The ceiling arched overhead into darkness, supported by embossed columns: scholars studying spinning orbs, guardians lifting a glowing heart, beings shaped like beasts and men walking side by side. Lanterns—long burned out—lined the walls, and in alcoves between the columns lay stacks of data spindles and leather-bound scripts, half-buried beneath years of ash. Kota sniffed at a fallen scroll. Ryo knelt to inspect the script—it was pre-Rapture, describing experiments in temporal harmonics, the "Chronological Convergence" meant to unify past and future. Then, scrawled in the margin, the words "Heart must anchor flow". His pulse quickened.

"The Heart... Kota's purpose." At the chamber's centre, on a low dais of obsidian, stood the Genesis Spindle—a crystalline recorder crackling with raw energy. It was taller than Ryo's shoulder, its spiralling rings etched with symbols that glowed silver. The fissures in its surface bled glowing strings into the air, each shimmering strand rippling like a living nerve.

Ryo stepped forward, awe warring with caution. He set his spear against the dais's edge and reverently touched the spindle's base. A pulse ran up his arm. He staggered back, heart racing—then steadied himself. The symbols brightened, casting the chamber in an ethereal light. Kota sat beside him, eyes reflecting the glow. Ryo pressed, what looked to be a small button on the spindle. Instantly, flickering images merged in the air: a ring of scientists in pristine labs, a vast engine humming with blue plasma, alarms blaring, voices crying out about breaches and failures. He heard only fragments:

"...exceeded safe threshold..."

"...activate contingency—the Heart..."

"...do it now or time collapses..."

The holo-probe sputtered and died. Ryo's jaw clenched. He backed away, gloved hand pressed to his chest.

"They gambled… with time itself." Beside the dais lay a battered holo-tablet. Ryo knelt and wiped ash from its screen. A map of underground levels flickered to life, showing tunnels and chambers beneath the city—one point circled in red: Level 7 – Convergence Chamber.

A timestamp glowed beneath: 10:10, the moment the world broke. He stepped back toward the platform, pausing to trace a symbol on its base—a stylized paw within a clock face, the emblem of the Timekeeper's Heart Prototype. He sketched it in charcoal on the dais's edge, committing the symbol to his own record. Kota looked up at him, as if acknowledging a shared destiny. A faint rumble shook the chamber. Dust cascaded from above. Symbols carved into the columns flickered and dimmed. Ryo's lamp beam blinked.

"Our time's up," he said, voice tight.

"These wards won't hold much longer."

Kota growled low. Ryo nodded and retraced his steps, guiding the dog through the aisles of spindles and scrolls. Each step stirred particles of ash that drifted like mournful ghosts. Behind them, the Genesis Spindle flared one last time, then began to crackle, shedding ribbons of unstable energy. Ryo paused at a side corridor. Through its archway he saw pale dawn light, dust particles swirling in its beam. Relief washed over him—freedom lay just beyond. He turned back to Kota.

"Let's go." They moved quickly now, stepping over broken holo-probes and abandoned data pads. Ryo's heart pounded as the rumble grew into a roar. The Genesis Spindle's ward collapsed in the distance, the crystal shards of its power leaping outward in a wave of displaced time-energy. They reached the corridor mouth—and froze. A distant metallic clang reverberated down the tunnel. Kota's anger rose; the dog snarled as shadows flickered along the walls.

Ryo narrowed his eyes. From the gloom stepped several figures in dark, patchwork armour—helmets visored in violet symbols, weapons held at the ready.

"Rift Hunters." he whispered.

Ryo whipped his spear into a two-handed grip. Kota crouched low, teeth bared. The corridor's distortions writhed around the newcomers, as though time itself leaned in to watch the confrontation. Ryo swallowed, shoulders tensing.

"Kota," he whispered,

"we knew this was coming." The Hunters advanced in silent, measured steps—eyes fixed on the exit.

Their leader raised a jagged shard-blade that pulsed with deadly intent and spoke through the haze:

"Hand over the Time Keeper, and you may yet leave with your life."

Ryo's pulse thundered as the words died on the respirator hiss of the commander before him. Kota's low, resonant growl rumbled through the corridor's distorted stillness. The first Rift Hunter reached out, a gauntlet crackling with shard-energy, aiming to seize the dog by the scruff.

Ryo raised his spear. Kota sprang forward, fur bristling, teeth bared. The corridor held its breath. And with that, the Revelation ended— and the Ambush began.

Chapter 18: Shadows in the Depths

Ryo lunged, spearpoint whistling. The commander's gauntlet unleashed a violet torrent that slammed him sideways into the wall. Pain flared across his ribs, but Ryo landed on his feet, teeth gritted. He spun and drove his spear into the commander's ankle guard. The energy bolt he'd fired twisted his lance into rainbow sparks, and his thrust unbalanced him. The commander staggered, his respirator clanking as he fought for breath. Kota snarled at his feet, tail lashing.

The dog lunged, teeth glinting as they caught the edge of his sleeve. He recoiled, discarded a clawed gauntlet that whipped against the stone, but Ryo was already pivoting to meet two flankers emerging from the gloom. One flanker brandished a trident–lance crackling with shard-light. The other hefted a gauss pistol that hummed in eerie anticipation. Ryo met them head-on, spear poised. The flanker with the pistol fired. A jagged bolt shredded the air inches from Ryo's cheek, scorching the wall. He charged, spear sweeping low; the butt slammed into the man's knee plate, sending him sprawling.

The other flanker leapt forward. Ryo ducked and retaliated with a savage upward jab, spear tip piercing the man's side. He gasped and toppled, his armour sputtering into ash. Ryo spun, backing toward the commander—only to find his revived, gauntlet-arm crackling.

He slammed him across the chest with a wave of shard-energy that threw him against a collapsed shelf. Data spindles tumbled like lethal marbles. Ryo's breath left him for a heartbeat. Kota barrelled into the commander's legs, clipping him off-balance. He cried out, stumbling. Ryo staggered up, eyes blazing.

"It ends here," he swore.

As Ryo advanced, the corridor's ancient ward-symbols carved into the floor flickered— struggling to hold reality in place against the vault's turbulent decay.

He glanced down: the pale magic beneath his boots teased at collapse. A ripple of chaos flickered through the air in front of them, hinting at a tear in the fabric of time. An idea sparked. Ryo glanced to his right: the corridor ended in a collapsed archway, shards of distortion drifting in the lamplight. A narrow fissure in the stone lunged open and closed with a silent hiss. A rift-gate, temporary but real. Ryo seized Kota's collar.

"Now, boy!" he barked.

Kota lunged at one of the Hunter's back, teeth clamping his armour seam. Ryo sprang past him, seizing his arm. He fought, clawing at him, but Ryo's grip was iron. He yanked him toward the fissure and with one mighty heave, shoved him off-balance—and into the maw of raw light and shadow.

His scream wrenched free and snapped shut as his feet slipped into the rift. The fissure cracked shut behind him with a resounding clang, the ward-symbol stones around it flaring to seal the open edge. Ryo stood panting, shoulder-deep in dust and shards. Kota shook himself, scattering ash. Ryo turned to face the flankers still advancing. One of the flankers—who had fired the gauss pistol—fired again, but Ryo parried the beam with his spear's shaft, sparks showering around them. He charged, thrusting low under the man's arm and driving the spear tip into the man's side.

The Hunter choked, pistol dropping. Ryo jerked the blade free; the man crumpled in a plume of violet dust. Two Hunters remained: the commander's lieutenant stumbling back to steady himself, wounded by Kota's charging tackle; the other, the commander who held a jagged shard-blade that pulsed with deadly intent.

They circled Ryo and Kota in a widening net. Ryo's chest burned with every breath, but he refused to yield. He planted his spear butt on the floor, pointed at the Hunters, and roared.

"I will not give in!" The lieutenant lunged. Ryo braced, letting the man's momentum carry him into the spear butt. Ryo twisted, using the haft as a lever, and threw the Hunter backward.

The man skidded across the symbol-etched floor, armour clattering, until he struck the corridor's fractured edge—and vanished with a wet crackle of displaced time. The commander remained—the man Ryo had knocked down. Now he tried to rise, blood seeping through his armour plating. Ryo whirled, eyes steel. Kota flashed in, teeth bared, and the final Hunter faced them alone. Ryo advanced, spearpoint low, silent menace in his gaze. The corridor's ceiling trembled, dust raining down. Ward-symbols flickered, threatening to collapse. Underfoot, the floor quivered as if ready to crack open. Ryo spoke softly, voice echoing:

"If you take one more step, you'll follow them." The Hunter's roar was half-defiance, half-fear. A shriek of shard-energy tore the concrete behind Ryo's head. Ryo dove aside, rolling forward and coming up behind him. He slid his spear under the Hunter's arm, lifting him off his feet. Kota flashed in again, tipping his balance, and Ryo spun, yanking the Hunter by his wrist toward the fissure's edge. The commander knocked, muzzle flaring. He glanced at the yawning rift and realized his fate too late. Ryo raised both hands and, with the dog's help, pushed him over the edge. A final scream echoed, then collapsed into silence as the rift-gate sealed in a flash of pale light and wards knocked back into place. Breathing hard, Ryo backed away from the sealed fissure.

His spear trembled in his grip. Kota sat panting, tail wagging once in triumphant relief. Behind them, the corridor lay empty of Hunters.

Ryo sank to one knee, pressing a hand to his chest. The vault's symbols around the rift glowed once more in a stabilizing pulse. He ran a hand over Kota's head.

"We did it," he whispered.

"All of them… gone."

The dog licked his palm, eyes bright with loyalty. Ryo stood, pulling the holo-tablet and shard canister from his pack. He slung them over his shoulder, spear ready once more. He turned and surveyed the corridor: shattered consoles, toppled shelves, footprints in ashen dust—proof of their struggle. But beyond the broken walls lay the broader darkness of the city's bones. Ryo exhaled, mind racing.

"We can't stay here," he said. Retracing their steps, Ryo and Kota navigated back through the Archives' shattered halls. They kept close to the walls, avoiding drifting shards of glass and the intermittent tremors that shook the ceiling. Symbols carved into pillars flickered in warning; he ignored them, pressing on toward the service stairs that would descend. At a landing halfway down the shaft, Ryo paused, listening.

Above him, the distant groan of shifting debris echoed. Below, he could almost hear the low rumble of the Convergence Chamber—distant but insistent. He crouched, checking the holo-map.

"Almost there," he whispered. He reached down to pet Kota's side.

"Ready?" Kota barked, stepping forward. They climbed the final flights, metal railing groaning under their weight. Ryo's muscles burned, but resolve drove him onward. At the bottom, a reinforced door marked Convergence Level – Restricted Access blocked the way. A keypad lay beside it, warped but functional. Ryo keyed in the override sequence gleaned from the holo-tablet. The door shuddered, then slid open with an atmospheric hiss. Beyond lay darkness pierced by the faint glow of a distant machine's pulsations. Ryo tightened his grip on the spear.

"Here we go." He stepped through the threshold—Kota at his side—and the door sealed behind them with a final thud. As the door closed, a new sound filled the chamber: a low, resonant pulse that matched Ryo's quickening heartbeat. He flicked on his lamp, revealing an immense vaulted hall. A colossal convergence engine stood in the centre—rings of corroded metal still spinning in half-life, pipes of blue plasma snaking toward its core.

The air hummed with unstable energy. Ryo stared, awed.

"The Convergence Chamber," he breathed. Kota moved beside him, nose twitching. The dog's dark eyes shone with quiet understanding: this was where Kota's origin had been forged, though its meaning remained hidden. Ryo squared his shoulders, stepping forward with spear levelled.

A burst of lightning outside rattled the massive windowpanes, illuminating the chamber in pale gold. The convergence engine trembled, gears grinding. Ryo raised a hand to shield his eyes. From the shadows beyond, a soft whistle echoed—an invitation or a challenge. Ryo's heart clenched. He gripped his spear tighter and took a single step toward the trembling heart of the machine.

The hall fell quiet, the tempest outside howling in its place, and in that stillness, the Rift revealed itself.

Chapter 19: The Last Thread

Ryo stood at the cliff of the great rift, the world between his feet splintered into jagged ledges and yawning chasms. Rain hissed against the cracked earth, turning the ash-flecked ground to slick mud. Above him, the sky churned in angry swirls of violet and gold—a storm-wracked wound in reality pulsing with chaotic energy. Every flash of lightning revealed the edges of the rift as living scars, the boundaries between decay and possibility. At his side, Kota sat perfectly still.

The dog's dark eyes were fixed on the turbulent chasm as if he understood the weight of the moment. Ryo pressed his hand against Kota's flank, feeling the steady thump of a heart that had guided them this far. He thought of every shard they had gathered, every secret uncovered, every battle fought. Now, at the journey's end, destiny demanded its final toll.

A distant rumble sent tremors along the ridge. Ryo braced himself. Kota rose and stepped forward, tail held rigid, gaze unwavering. Ryo swallowed against the sick knot in his chest.

"Kota…" he whispered.

A soft footfall from behind made him spin. Kaori emerged from the shadows under a collapsed overpass, her dark cloak plastered to her shoulders. The rain washed pale streaks across her cheeks, but her golden eyes burned bright with ancient sorrow and resolute purpose. She moved with quiet grace, though the wind threatened to whip her from her feet.

"Ryo," she breathed, as though greeting both him and the storm itself. He swallowed.

"Kaori… you're here…"

She came closer, boots sinking into mud. Her gaze lingered on the storm before she reached out her hand.

"Hold out your hand." He hesitated, heart pounding too fast to trust his own breath. But Kaori's sorrowful determination urged him forward. Slowly, Ryo extended his palm. Kaori placed her hand over his, her touch surprisingly warm against the cold, driving rain.

"Close your eyes," she instructed.

Ryo obeyed. The moment his eyelids fell, a surge of energy—undeniable, brutal—crashed through him. Veins of power rippled beneath his skin, and the world around him dissolved like ink in water. Kota's whine faded into silence; the storm's roar was replaced by a single heartbeat, steady and resonant. When the light receded, Ryo found himself somewhere else.

He stood in a cavernous research facility that bore no scars—not a single crack in its metallic walls, not a drop of rain on its immaculately polished floor. The ceiling soared above in a grid of white lights that glowed like an artificial sky.

Scientists in lab coats moved with urgent purpose, their voices hushed but frantic, echoing along catwalks rimmed with chrome.

In the centre of the hall rose the Convergence Engine—a structure of spinning rings and humming pipes, each ring inscribed with equations and glyphs that pulsed with raw, unstable energy. Tubes of transparent alloy carried streams of blazing blue plasma in and out, feeding the engine's hungry core.

"They thought they could control time," Kaori's voice floated beside him, though she was nowhere to be seen.

"They wanted to rewrite history—to erase the mistakes of the past and create a perfect future." Ryo moved forward, boots silent on the metal grating. He circled the engine, reading the flickering readouts: CONTINGENCY: HEART PROTOCOL. He swallowed hard. The scientists clustered around a holo-screen displaying global data—wars undone, famine reversed, tragedies erased. Their excitement was electric. A scientist gasped.

"We're within safe parameters. Prepare to activate the Rewind Sequence." Another shook her head.

"No, we push for Complete Rewrite. This is our chance—" The first scientist grabbed her arm.

"Don't let ambition blind you! We have the Heart Protocol as insurance if things go wrong."

"The Heart Protocol?" the woman repeated. Her eyes darted to Ryo before he adjusted his visor. No one here saw him; he was invisible in this memory. Ryo felt a pull toward a side chamber. He stepped through sliding doors, leaving the engine's chorus of hums behind. Inside was a small cradle—cradled within wires of glowing crystal. And within it, curled like a pup deep in sleep, lay a newborn Shiba Inu, fur shining with pale light. Ryo froze. Kota whined, stepping forward.

"They..." Kaori's voice trembled.

"They didn't just break time. They created something new." The holo-display on the cradle blinked: LIVING FRAGMENT: TIMEKEEPER'S HEART. Ryo's breath caught. He pressed a hand to the transparent wall. The pup's eyes fluttered open. Within them danced starlight and storms.

"They formed him," Kaori whispered,

"to anchor the chaos they themselves unleashed." Lightning flashed overhead. The two scientists returned to the cradle, one tenderly cradling the pup. Outside, alarms began to wail. The ringed pipes around the engine convulsed in overload. Sparks flew. Tremors shook the floor. Ryo stumbled backward. He raised a hand, dazed. Then—everything went wrong. A blinding white light blasted from the core of the Convergence Engine. Vines of raw time-energy lashed outward like furious serpents, ripping through floors, vaulting into upper catwalks, scattering scientists like rag dolls.

The alarms fractured into static cries. Glass domes above shattered, and Ryo felt a vacuum rip at his chest. He stumbled through the wreckage, visions alternating with reality: one moment he saw bodies frozen in mid-step, the next, ground tremors erased their forms, leaving only dust. A woman's scream caught in his throat, then evaporated.

Through the storm, he glimpsed the pup's cradle shuddering under the strain. Wires snapped. Crystal shards floated in the air. And then Ryo saw it—the precise moment Kota was born. From the heart of the implosion, a figure of raw temporal energy condensed into living form. Soft, crystalline shapes merged into four sturdy paws, a curled tail, and a small trembling head.

The pup lay curled in the swirling storm, formed not by birth but by the furious dance of time's raw fabric. Ryo's vision was frozen on that creature's first breath—a breath drawn in defiance of annihilation.

"They created him not to destroy time, but to preserve it," Kaori's voice echoed as the vision wavered.

"A living fragment of the Heart they no longer understood." A lone scientist, white coat stained by smudged ash and flickering temporal residue, knelt on splintered metal flooring. In her arms she cradled the tiny, ethereal pup: Kota. Her hands trembled as she pressed him close to her chest, eyes brimming with tears that caught the harsh glow of the convergence engine's dying light. Around them the world fractured in storms of raw energy, yet she remained a sanctuary of calm, rocking him gently.

"He was the last pure fragment of time," Kaori's voice whispered behind Ryo's closed eyelids, and the scientist's lips moved without sound:

"My heart... my world... lives in you." In that moment, Kota nuzzled her throat as if offering solace. The vision faded, but the echo of her love—a promise forged in chaos—lingered like a soft pulse beneath Ryo's ribs. A blast wave struck. Ryo's hands flew to his ears. The world exploded outward, and he was swept into darkness. Ryo gasped and tumbled backward, reemerging at the edge of the rift—rain lashing again, wind screaming. His eyes burned, but he saw Kaori standing before him, her hand still in his.

She withdrew her palm. Ryo blinked. The memory vanished, leaving only the storm's fury. Kota nosed at Ryo's hand.

The dog's flank brushed against him, warm and real. Ryo staggered to his feet.

"Kota…" His voice shook with wonder and anguish. Kaori watched him, expression solemn.

"Now you know." Ryo sank to his knees.

"He was never just a companion. He was the Heart." His fingers trembled as they traced the outline of the shard in his pack.

"He was made for this." Kaori knelt beside him.

"Yes. And only he can mend what was broken." Ryo closed his eyes. Each thunderclap echoed the rift's ragged breath. He thought of every battle they had fought, every Survivor they had helped. Now the final act awaited. Kaori's voice cut through the storm, steady but trembling at its edges. Raindrops streaked down her face, but in the shimmer of the storm light, Ryo realized they weren't only from the sky.

Her tears mixed with the rain, vanishing as quickly as they fell, yet the sorrow in her eyes remained unmistakable.

"It is time," she whispered, the words heavy with both grief and inevitability.

"No," Ryo whispered, looking up at Kaori.

"There must be another way." His eyes burned with desperation.

"I can't lose him." Kaori placed a hand on his shoulder, gentle but unyielding.

"He won't be lost. He knows his purpose. He has always known." Ryo shook his head, struggling against the truth. Kaori's gaze held him firm. She pointed toward the rift's swirling core.

"This is where he must go." Ryo's chest tightened.

"I… I understand." For a long moment, he stared at the abyss. Kota sat beside him, silhouette outlined by the storm's flicker. The dog turned his gaze to Ryo, eyes shining with quiet resolve. Tears streamed down Ryo's face as he pressed his forehead against Kota's soft, warm head.

Every touch, every gentle lick from Kota, recalled a thousand cherished moments: the way the little pup had once curled up in his lap, the countless nights they had shared beneath a sky filled with hopeless stars, and the rare, shining moments of laughter amid despair. All those memories were precious beyond measure.

The rift began to intensify. The unstable vortex, once a distant threat, now surged with a fierce, unrelenting energy. Its chaotic light bathed the world in a spectral glow, and the roar of its power became deafening. Ryo's heart ached with a grief so profound it threatened to shatter him completely, yet amid the pain, a quiet determination began to emerge.

He knew that to protect the future—to allow the possibility of a new dawn—he would have to accept this sacrifice, as painful as it was. With a trembling voice, Ryo whispered,

"I love you, Kota. I promise, I will carry you in my heart forever. Your sacrifice… your love will be the light that guides us through the darkness."

His words, raw and broken, were a solemn vow to honour every moment they had shared. Slowly, with a deliberate grace that belied the magnitude of the moment, Kota rose from Ryo's embrace.

The dog stepped forward toward the churning vortex of the rift, his every movement displaying an ethereal calm.

His fur shimmered as if injected with an inner radiance, and the air around him pulsed in response—like a silent chorus echoing the heartbeat of the universe.

Ryo, unable to tear his eyes away, watched as Kota turned his gaze toward the storm, his expression serene and determined.

Kaori's eyes filled with tears as she took a step closer, her voice barely above a whisper.

"Kota's power—his very essence—is meant to heal the rift, to restore the order of time. This is his destiny, and by accepting it, he offers all of us a chance at a future."

Ryo's vision blurred as he fought to hold back the surge of grief. The world around him seemed to slow, the distant thunder fading into a soft murmur. In that moment of stillness, as if time itself were offering a final, fragile pardon, Ryo gazed deeply into Kota's eyes. There, he saw not only a silent farewell but also an unyielding spark—a promise that even in sacrifice, love endures.

"Don't leave me," Ryo pleaded once more, his voice trembling as if it might break. But in Kota's gaze, Ryo found the courage to accept the truth. He knew that in order to mend the world, he must let go. Ryo's vision blurred with tears. He rose, hands outstretched.

"Kota!" Kota paused and looked back, eyes gleaming with something ancient and knowing. Ryo's heart shattered in that single, unspoken farewell. With one final bound, Kota plunged into the storm of light and shadow.

Ryo fell to his knees as the storm roared. The rift's howling grew deafening, then paused—as though holding its breath. A final flash of brilliance blinded him.

Then—silence. Ryo blinked. Rain tapped softly on his face. The wind had stilled. Above the chasm, clouds parted just enough to reveal a pale sun hanging low on the horizon. Its light seemed tender, as if afraid to disturb the calm.

The rift's edges glowed with a gentle pulse—no longer violent, but rhythmic, a heartbeat once more. Time, it seemed, was settling into a new breath. Ryo felt hollow and alive all at once. He stared at the calm wound in reality, waiting for a sign of Kota. But there was only the rift's soft luminescence. Amber light pooled on the cracked earth.

Ryo closed his eyes, breathing deeply as the world exhaled around him. From the chasm came a distant echo—an echo of a heartbeat. His chest tightened. Hope, he realized, could still be born in silence. Kaori knelt beside him, her hand warm and steady on his shoulder.

"Your love for him will never fade, Ryo. His light now lives on in the fabric of time. Though you cannot see him, his presence will guide you, and his sacrifice will serve as a beacon to mend the wounds of our shattered world."

He turned to Kaori, the rain had cleared from her cloak, but her eyes glistened with tears she refused to shed.

"He did it," Ryo said, voice barely above a whisper.

"He saved time." Kaori nodded,

"And now the world will remember." Ryo folded his hands, as if in prayer. For a moment, the sky held its breath. Then the sun broke free, casting long, golden fingers across the rift.

Ryo closed his eyes to let the warmth wash over him. In that moment, he felt Kota's presence—steady, eternal—woven into the restored heartbeat of time itself. The rift, now stabilized into a gentle, rhythmic pulse, radiated a soft glow that seemed to wash over the ruins like a blessing. The chaotic storm had given way to a quiet, almost sacred stillness—a moment where the immense loss was tempered by the promise of renewal. In the space where Kota had vanished, Ryo felt a subtle warmth—a lingering echo of the dog's love that now intertwined with the very energy of time.

For hours, Ryo remained at the edge of the rift, his grief raw and his heart heavy with the magnitude of the sacrifice. The world around him seemed to hold its breath, the wind a soft murmur, the rain gently falling. In that fragile silence, Ryo could almost hear Kota's familiar bark in the rustle of the leaves and the whisper of the wind—a reminder that even in sacrifice, love endures beyond the physical realm. Kaori's voice, soft and steady, eventually broke the silence.

"Ryo, it is time to rise. Though tonight is filled with sorrow, remember that Kota's sacrifice has gifted us with hope—a chance to rebuild and to mend the broken strands of time. He lives on in every heartbeat, in every quiet moment of beauty that emerges from the ruins."

Ryo slowly rose to his feet, each movement a painful reminder of his loss. He wiped away his tears with trembling hands, and in the distance, he saw the first hints of dawn creeping over the horizon—a new day dawning in a world forever changed by sacrifice.

"I will honour you, Kota," he vowed, voice firm yet laced with sorrow.

"Your love will guide me, and I will fight to restore the future."

Chapter 20: Beyond the Silence

Ryo stood on the sodden earth, drenched by the clearing rain and the weight of unspoken sorrow. The great rift lay calm before him now—its jagged edges glowing with a soft, steady pulse that spoke of healing. The storm had passed; only the faint hiss of residual energy drifted upward into a sky slowly brightening with dawn. Kota's sacrifice still echoed in every fibre of his being—an emptiness he could neither fill nor ignore.

The world had shifted on its axis, and he felt detached. A soft footfall made him look up. Kaori stood at the rim of the chasm, her cloak drying in the new light. Her golden eyes met his—tender and grave. She approached without a word and stood beside him.

Ryo did not notice when the last winds of the storm died away, leaving only the gentle rustle of ash against stone. He did not feel Kaori's hand on his shoulder until her voice, low and steady, broke the hush.

"Ryo."

He looked at her, eyes red-rimmed.

"It's over," he rasped. Kaori shook her head.

"Not yet."

She drew a deep breath, as if drawing strength from the fragile dawn.

"I promised you the truth. Now that the rift is sealed—for now—you deserve to hear it."

Ryo's gaze dropped back to the fissure. He whispered,

"I don't know what's left for me."

"First," Kaori said, "you must understand who I am—and what this world has become."

"I am a Time Weaver," she began.

"One of the last of my kind." Ryo's brow furrowed.

"A... what?" Kaori offered him a small, sad smile.

"Time Weavers are neither gods nor sorcerers. We are guardians—custodians of the timeline. Our purpose is to guide the flow of time, to guard against corruption, and to preserve the integrity of reality." She turned her gaze to the tranquil rift.

"After the Time Rapture, many lost faith in time's continuity. We stayed behind the scenes, mending tears, protecting what remained."

Ryo listened, absorbing each word as though tasting medicine—bitter but necessary.

"Why hide? Why wait?"

"There were too few of us," Kaori explained.

"And the forces that fractured time were too powerful. We could not confront the disaster head-on. Instead, we became watchers—searching for the spark that could restore balance. That spark was Kota."

"All this time...", Ryo whispered.

Kaori nodded.

"I watched you and Kota from afar, guiding you toward each fragment of truth. I nudged you to the Mirage Village, the Timeless City, the Archives... always to prepare you for this moment." She paused, letting the dawn's light trace her features.

"I never meant to leave you in the dark, but I had to wait until the time was right." Ryo shook his head slowly.

"You could have told me." Kaori touched his arm.

"Some truths demand proof, not promise. You needed to see Kota's power, to trust him before understanding his origin. Only then could you accept what must come next." Kaori led Ryo a few paces back from the rift's edge, where a rough outcrop offered relative shelter. She knelt on a flat stone and motioned for him to sit. Ryo perched beside her, shoulders tense.

"Listen," she said, her voice a soft hum.

"Before the Rapture, the world believed in time's sanctity—an unbroken river carrying memory, history, and destiny. Some feared what lay beyond its banks; others believed they could channel it. A secret council of scientists and mystics conspired to harness temporal energy— to rewrite history's darkest chapters, eradicate war, famine, plague. They built the Convergence

Engine to bend time to their will." Ryo closed his eyes, recalling the vision in the Archives.

"They almost succeeded," he murmured. Kaori continued.

"Yes. But humanity cannot master what it barely understands. When they activated the machine, the energy back-reacted, fracturing the connection. The fabric of time tore apart in an instant—history looped, futures shattered, and the world fell into chaos."

Lightning flickered far off, as though echoing her words. Ryo flinched.

"Afterwards," Kaori said,

"we attempted to contain the fallout. We wove protective enchantments around key nodes—libraries, labs, vaults—places where temporal data was stored. But the Rift Hunters betrayed us." Ryo looked at her.

"The Rift Hunters were Time Weavers?" Kaori shook her head.

"They were once like us—engineers and scholars who believed that time should be controlled, not preserved. They defected, taking forbidden knowledge and blending it with the darkest energies in the rift. The Council exiled them into the fracture—a prison of looping chaos. But they did not perish. They adapted, became twisted by the rift's power, and waged war from within, seeking a path back to reality."

Ryo's fists clenched.

"They wanted to use Kota. They tried to break him, to harness his gift." Kaori's gaze was fierce.

"They were relentless. Only Kota's essence—his will—kept them at bay. He anchored the fragments of time we couldn't hope to control." She took a breath.

"And now", her voice broke,

"he is gone." Ryo stared at the rift.

"But he saved us." Kaori nodded.

"Yes. He gave his life to seal the wound. But the fracture remains fragile. That is why I offered you a choice."

Kaori paused, her breath catching in the sudden hush. Ryo's eyes searched hers.

"You saw a lone scientist holding Kota," she whispered, voice soft with memory.

"That scientist... was me." Ryo's head snapped up.

"You?" Kaori drew her knees to her chest, wrapping her arms around them as if bracing against an old storm.

"I volunteered when the Convergence Protocol began to fail. They needed someone to protect the Heart Protocol—someone who believed in what they were building, even as it unraveled. I stayed with him through the collapse, shielding him from the worst of the backlash." She closed her eyes.

"I felt every fracture of time that tore around us. I carried him into the world they broke— because he was the only thing left worth preserving." Ryo reached out, trembling.

"You held him… you held Kota." Kaori's hand found his.

"I held him first. And now, you hold his legacy." A hush fell. The world beyond lay quiet, the rift's pulsations a gentle murmur rather than a howl. Kaori reached into her cloak and drew out a slim, leather-bound journal—tattered edges, pages yellowed with age.

"This is the Chronicle of the Time Weavers," she said, pressing it into Ryo's hands.

"It holds our vows, our failures, and our methods of guidance." Ryo sat down, opened it, running fingertips over the elegant script and diagrams of warded signals.

"I can't replace Kota," he whispered.

"I can barely save myself." Kaori sat beside him, close enough that their shoulders touched.

"I know. You need not replace him—you need only choose how to honour his sacrifice. You have two paths." Ryo looked up.

"What are they?" Kaori's eyes shone with dawn's first light.

"First: you can return to the flow of time—to the life you once knew, with this knowledge in your heart. You might live a quiet life, away from the burden of torn timelines. Kota's memory would be your guide, and you would guard this world in your own way—through your choices, not your powers." She paused. Ryo's heart thudded in his ears.

"And second," Kaori continued,

"you can join the Time Weavers. Learn our ways. Help me and the few of us left to protect the timeline, to prevent another Rapture. It would mean training, sacrifice, perhaps living apart from the world—to heal its wounds rather than share its joys directly." Ryo closed the journal with a soft snap.

"A guardian… like you." Kaori nodded.

"Not control, but stewardship. To shepherd time, so no one else can exploit it."

Ryo pressed the journal to his chest. He thought of Kota—steadfast, luminous, formed in chaos to preserve hope. He thought of the shard's faint glow and the stable heartbeat of the rift. Kaori waited, her hand on his shoulder, silent as the first birdsong of morning. Ryo rose, journal in hand. He stood at the rift's brink once more, watching the light fade into brilliance. Time, for the first time in decades, seemed patient—an ally rather than a predator. Kaori remained seated, head bowed. Ryo returned to her side.

"I will not walk away, not now. Not after everything." Kaori's head lifted.

"You choose…" Ryo nodded.

"I choose to stand guard. To keep the promise Kota made with his sacrifice. If the Time Weavers exist to protect what he died for, then I will join them." A relief like sunrise bloomed in Kaori's eyes. She rose gracefully, offering her hand. Ryo took it.

"I will teach you," she said.

"Our vows, our rituals, the weaving. Together, we will guard the streams of time." Ryo inhaled the crisp air—tang of ash, of rain, of new beginnings. The journal felt weighty but not burdensome. Kaori guided him in the first ritual: a simple warding circle, stones etched with symbols that glowed faintly as Ryo traced them. He whispered the oath of the Time Weavers:

"I vow to honour the flow of time, to safeguard memory and future alike, to stand against corruption, and to shield reality from those who would bend it to ruin." His voice wavered, but each word settled into the earth, resonating like a heartbeat. When he finished, the stones pulsed once, then settled into a steady light. Kaori smiled, a gentle curve of triumph and relief.

"Welcome, Ryo, Guardian of Time."

They stood side by side at the empty dawn. Kota's absence lay between them like an open wound, yet beneath his loss pulsed a promise—a quiet rhythm that would guide them. Ryo looked at the still, healing rift.

"He's with us," he murmured. Kaori nodded.

"In every moment we protect, in every stitch we weave, Kota's essence endures. Time remembers its champions." Ryo closed his eyes, feeling the first warmth of sunrise on his face. The rift, the shards, the lost Archives—all were chapters left behind. Ahead lay a path woven by memory, by sacrifice, and by thawed fragments of hope. He opened his eyes on Kaori's calm face—the face of a teacher, a guide, and now, his mentor in the infinite dance of time. Together, they turned from the rift's edge.

Step by measured step, they walked toward a future uncharted but protected—bearing the legacy of the Timekeeper's Heart in their choices and their vows. Ryo reached into his pouch and drew out the tiny shard reminder—a sliver of blue light that pulsed once in his palm. He held it aloft, and the shard glowed bright before dimming again—an echo of Kota's heart.

At the corner of his vision, he saw movement. A slender silhouette perched atop a moss-grown stone: a Shiba Inu, fur softly glowing in the dawn, eyes bright with recognition. Kota. Ryo's heart thundered. He dropped to one knee, chest tightening with hope and disbelief. The dog's head tilted, ears pricked, as if greeting an old friend. In that single, whispered moment, the weight of loss gave way to something gentler: a promise kept across time.

"Kota?" Ryo's voice trembled.

The Shiba inclined his head once, then bounded down the slope, paws light on the earth. Ryo rose, tears glinting in his eyes, and took a step forward—then another. He and Kaori moved together, drawn toward the living echo of the Heart. As Kota reached them, he nuzzled Ryo's hand, steady and warm.

Ryo knelt, wrapping his arms around his friend. The world around them shimmered with the first true light of tomorrow, but in that quiet embrace, time itself held its breath—honouring the bond that had saved it. And as Ryo held Kota close, he whispered into the golden dawn,

"Together, we'll guide this world into its first true morning."

Manufactured by Amazon.ca
Bolton, ON